Lies and Deceit

Lies and Deceit

The Story of Henrietta Fogg

Brian Mackenzie

Archway Publishing books may be ordered through booksellers or by contacting:

Archway Publishing
1663 Liberty Drive
Bloomington, IN 47403
www.archwaypublishing.com
844-669-3957

ISBN: 978-1-6657-2115-8 (sc)
ISBN: 978-1-6657-2116-5 (e)

Library of Congress Control Number: 2022905972

Print information available on the last page.

Archway Publishing rev. date: 04/11/2022

*To all who struggle with the day-to-day
woes of life. You are not alone.*

Acknowledgements

I'd like to thank my partner and sister for reading my manuscript. If it weren't for them, I wouldn't have pushed myself to get it published. I appreciate the time and feedback provided. Words can't express how much that means. I'd like to thank all my family and friends who continued to push me to get this book published. I'd like to thank everyone who offered to assist me on this journey. I love you all dearly.

1

Meet the Family

y name is Henrietta Fogg. Everyone calls me Ri, except my close family, who call me Etta. Henri-fucking-etta. I was born in the 1980s, yet my name is Henrietta. What were my parents thinking? I was born in Rocket City, Pond Beat, Alabama. That's it. They're from Alabama. That's why they named me Henrietta. My light-skinned, pretty ass arrived in the seven o'clock hour of the morning. I've learned that doesn't dictate whether you're a morning person because I don't like getting up early. I'm a total bitch in the morning. Talk to me after noon.

Pond Beat County is home to the Space Center, Pond Beat Arsenal, the University of Alabama in Rocket City (UARC), and Normal University (NU). I'm a proud Alabamian who believes Alabama the Beautiful is an accurate description of my home state because of the mountains, greenery, and bodies of water. I was raised on the northwest side of Rocket City. When people ask me where I'm from, I gladly tell them, "I'm from the Nawfside of Rocket City, Alabama. Fo' Seven!" The north side is known to be a tad bit ghetto. We lived right across the street from a trap house.

I'm an eighties baby born under the best zodiac sign, Leo. I'm hot like fire, so it's only natural for me to be a summer baby born under this glorious fire sign. Leos are known to be loyal, so please don't cross us unless you want to hear us roar. If you make me roar, then you just might catch these paws. I'm an early eighties baby, so I'm not a millennial. I'm a xennial, on the cusp of Gen X and millennials. We know how to operate without being fully dependent on the Internet or the Internet of things. We don't get sad because we don't have enough likes on our social media statuses. We know how to go out and have a good time without being on our phones the entire time. We don't have to film everything and have it viewed on Snapchat.

I have six beautiful siblings. Yes, my mother gave birth to seven children, and I'm child number four. The Bible mentions being fruitful and multiplying. Living in the Bible Belt and growing up in the church, my mother took that to heart. I guess all she did was go to church and have sex. My mother told me she always wanted a daughter, and she finally got me. God bless her. Be careful what you wish for because you just might get it. Although my mother prayed for a daughter, I was her only daughter, which means I have three older and three younger brothers. Needless to say, I was the favorite child.

By the time I was born, all my biological grandparents were deceased except for my maternal grandmother, Charity. She married Oscar, my step-grandfather. He was the only grandpa I knew. Oscar was nice, but I feel as if he was disliked by default because he wasn't our biological grandpa.

My older cousins said things like, "He ain't my granddaddy." As long as my grandma was happy, I felt that was all that should have mattered. Maybe I also felt that way because I didn't know my biological grandfather. I didn't have the close ties the others had. Charity was a stern woman who didn't hesitate to say what was on her mind, but she also had a huge heart. She was known as the candy lady in her neighborhood. She sold all kinds of snacks.

My mom sent us to Grandma's occasionally to visit as well as stay overnight. Grandma didn't like when I spent the night because I peed in the bed. I was so embarrassed. It's not like I was doing it on purpose. We got to consume the snacks she had, but she limited them. She gave us Moon Pies, which I despised. I don't understand how anyone likes them. However, she also made Kool Pops. Those were my favorite. They were the old-school kind, where you froze the Kool-Aid inside a cup versus the new-school Kool Pops that you purchase in a box from the grocery store. Outside of them just being delicious, they were probably my favorite because they cooled me off.

Certain areas of Grandma's house were extremely hot. It probably felt better to be outside. She kept the front and back doors open, but the storm doors were closed. I'm sure the air conditioning couldn't circulate properly with those doors open. The sun beamed hard on the glass storm doors. One time she cooked us breakfast and burned the bacon. The heat from the stove and the smell from the burned bacon did not mix well with the heat in the house. The small kitchen table was right next to the back door, so eating there during the day wasn't fun. The living room was right next to the kitchen, so the heat traveled.

Grandma Charity and my mother, Cheryl, didn't get along well. I feel like it was because they were too much alike, but I never figured out if that was the sole reason. They were both known as being mean and stuck in their ways, but they both had huge hearts. They loved to give. They believed that if you blessed others, the blessings would return tenfold. Neither one was the best cook. Grandma burned bacon, and Mama doesn't season food well. It was like she was cooking for diabetics. I didn't realize how bland her food was until I was able to taste food from outside of her home. It was like night and day. I tried to give her a tip on adding some flavor to her collard greens, and she got offended. I won't do that again. She acted as if I had given her a tip on how to suck dick. She was furious.

Mama has a unique look for a black woman. She is fair-skinned with red hair and freckles (I suppose she's considered a redbone). Her eyes also change colors. She got married to my daddy at an early age—she was sixteen. I feel that was the best opportunity for her to get out of her mother's house. Regardless of how she felt about her mother, she ensured her kids had a relationship with their grandmother.

Mama's father, Lee Mallory Sr., died a few years before I was born. He was a reverend of a church, and my mother followed in his footsteps by being the pastor of her church. She also followed in her parents' footsteps by having a lot of kids. My mother had twelve siblings. According to her siblings, she was a weird child who didn't want to socialize or play with them or their cousins. She always played by herself. Although she did not finish high school, Mama is very business savvy and quite good with finances. She made sure we were taken care of by any means necessary. However, she was also strict and never let us do much of anything. Whenever we asked if we could do something, have something, or go somewhere, 98 percent of the time the answer was no.

My father, David, was head over heels for my mother. He spoiled her and let her do whatever she wanted. He gave her his paycheck when payday arrived. He spoiled us too, but only if my mother approved or wouldn't find out about it. I was Daddy's little girl, so I usually got what I wanted if I cried. He didn't beat our asses unless Mama asked him to.

He didn't talk about his family much. Hell, he barely talked about anything at all. He was known for going to work, working on the family vehicles, working on the house, cooking, watching wrestling, and sleeping. He was also known for smoking cigarettes and drinking beer and liquor, but that has ceased. The only time he left the house was to go to work or the store. I recall when we went to the ABC store after school. I thought it was a school supply store. Later, I learned it's a liquor store. Now it makes sense why we were never able to get out of the car to go inside. It's now one of my favorite stores—go figure!

My dad's parents were already deceased by the time I was born. He had two brothers, John and Saul. I only recall face-to-face interactions with one. Saul always called the house to wish us a happy birthday days before our birthdays arrived. It's definitely the thought that counts. I met one of my dad's aunts, Flordee, when we went to her house in River City, Tennessee. She bought us, a family of nine, a meal from Church's Chicken that fed a family of five. I guess it was not her fault that her nephew had an army of kids she couldn't afford to feed. We made do with what she provided, even though we were still hungry. I don't recall her having any kids. If she did, it was never mentioned.

Just like Grandma Charity, she also burned bacon at breakfast. She tasted the bacon and said, "Ooh wee! This bacon shole is coonchy." (Translation: "This bacon sure is crunchy.") She had a dog named Loo Loo that she simply adored. That was the first and last visit I recall seeing my great-aunt Flordee.

My eldest brother, Andrew, whom we call Andy, is Mama's little helper. I don't know if that automatically comes along with being the first child, or it's something he just likes doing. He'll do anything to ensure he makes Mama proud, even if it jeopardizes his peace of mind. He stepped in when Mama was away on business. He made sure we woke up on time for school, had meals, got dressed in a presentable manner, and stayed out of trouble.

My dad worked twelve-hour shifts, so he wasn't able to assist most of the time. A lot of my friends and classmates thought Andy was my daddy because he was always present when my mother was out of town. I consider him a second father.

He just says, "That's what big brothers do." In spite of all his chores around the house, he was able to successfully graduate from high school. He set the standard for the rest of us to follow due to neither of our parents achieving this goal.

After high school, he lived with us for a long time. His first girlfriend came over on her bike with her biking tights on. Mama was funny about who she allowed coming inside the house, so they had to talk outside on the porch. I was right out there with them, being nosy. I wondered if her biking tights hurt her coochie, because they sure looked like they did. She also had lipstick on her teeth. I don't know what he saw in her. For whatever reason, that relationship didn't work out. However, one monkey don't stop no show. He currently has two kids, so he's moving along just fine.

Jackson, better known as Jack, the second oldest, is just awful for no reason. He's always mean. It's like he had a rough life. Maybe he did and I was just too young to see it. He tortured us. He made us pop his acne and clip his toenails. If we didn't, he punched us in the chest or arm. He used to frog us in the shoulder area hard. We hit each other while he drove me to school. I got out of the car crying on my way to my first class. I was so embarrassed.

When I was younger, he got into trouble for letting us get into some bullshit while he was supposed to be watching us. Our neighbors had a Slip 'N' Slide, that waterslide toy you filled with water. It got slippery, allowing us to slide down. We wanted one, but we were told we couldn't have one.

So we took the pillows from the lawn furniture and lined them up in the living room. The pillows were very slick. I'm not sure what type of material they were made out of. I slid down the pillows mouth first into the leg of a table. I knocked out my two front teeth. Jack got his ass beat for that event. Maybe that was why he was rude all the time. Honestly, I think it's just his nature.

On the bright side, he worked at restaurants that had food I enjoyed, and he brought me some. My favorite was the hot wings. I've always been a fan of chicken of any kind. You'd think since he worked in restaurants he would have a soft spot for restaurant workers. He does not. Anytime something is wrong with his food order, he never asks for a replacement in a nice manner. It's always with an attitude. It's disrespectful and embarrassing.

Despite the dynamic of our relationship during my childhood, we're still close. I guess it was just tough love. He dropped out of high school. His mind just wasn't in the game. He was always skipping class and getting suspended. He dated one of his coworkers. After a few years, they got married. They stayed in the house with us for a short time. He eventually enlisted in the US Army, and they moved to Germany for a couple of years. I missed him a lot. We wrote each other letters all the time, and I still have them. I took German in high school thinking I'd be able to visit him while he was there. That never happened. He currently has two spoiled-ass children. In addition to being the first sibling to leave the nest, he's also the first to reach grandparent status.

Being the only girl had its pros and cons. Shawn, child number three, used to torture me. He quickly learned I was spoiled because I'm the only girl. He knew I always got whatever I wanted, so he used me to ask for things when he wanted them. If he wanted to go play over the neighbor's house, I had to say we wanted to go play. If he wanted a toy, I had to say we wanted a toy. If I didn't comply, there were consequences. I recall being chased by him with a knife because I refused to do what he asked of me. I ran and hid in a closet. I pulled the door handle toward me so he couldn't open the door. He slid the knife under the door, trying to cut my feet.

He always stayed in some kind of trouble. If a problem child had to be chosen, he easily received the title. He didn't graduate from high school either. He sneaked girls into the house. One time, he sneaked a girl in, and I told him I was going to tell. He knew I wouldn't, so he didn't care. I went outside and hosed them through his bedroom window. I guess I was a cockblocker that day.

He's been to jail multiple times, and I got caught up with him once. We walked around the mall, and he decided to steal some clothes. I didn't do anything wrong, but since I was with him, I went to the detention center. Hopefully, that was my first and last time being in handcuffs. I knew my mom was going to beat my ass, but she felt sorry for me.

In addition to the bad behavior, he also has a bunch of baby mamas. They all come with their drama. I've always heard that your kids give you ten times the hell that you gave your parents. I think the majority of his kids do exactly that. I'll say three out of the five give him a run for his money. Despite all the craziness, we're close. We party harder than any of my other siblings. He's also the only one who got the changing eye color trait from our mom. Maybe the changing eye color represents a change in personality. If that's the case, I'll be fine with my light brown eyes.

My unofficial twin, Marcus, whom we call Marc, is child number five. I call him my twin because we share the same birthday, although we're two years apart. We tricked people into thinking we were twins. I told people he was two years behind because he flunked twice. He told people I was a gifted student, so I was able to move up two grades. We look so much alike. People say I look like him with a wig on. He was the snitch of the family and tattled all the time. It was like he got a natural high from it. We always battled on our birthday. He wrote his name on the calendar, and I scratched it out and then wrote my name in the remaining space. It also happened the other way around depending on who got to the calendar first.

We had to share certain birthday gifts. One year, we got a Power Wheel. It was a two-seater, and we could've easily ridden together. However, we fought over who got to drive as well as whether we could ride solo.

Marc is extremely intelligent. He never got in trouble in or outside school. He was the first of the family to graduate from college. He married his college sweetheart, who was my classmate. I also worked with his wife at my very first job, which was before they got married. They have a child who is extremely spoiled, smart, and hilarious.

The sixth child, Lyndon, also known as Lyn, was extremely quiet growing up. He acts just like Daddy. He and Andy are the only children who got Daddy's chocolate complexion. All the rest of us are light brights. Lyn always minds his business; he doesn't care for unnecessary drama. He's extremely outspoken, just like Grandma Charity.

He doesn't mess with anyone unless he's provoked. One summer, my cousins came down from Grind City, Tennessee. Cousin George kept picking on Lyn. Lyn tried to fight him. He chased George around outside the house in the rain. He eventually caught up with George in the backyard and beat his ass. George didn't bother him for the rest of the trip. It's always the quiet ones you have to watch.

Lyn eventually got married and had kids. He still keeps to himself to include not coming around the family much. He demands things be done his way regardless of how you feel about it, especially if the other way is going to waste his time or bring negative energy. If we want to meet up, we have to meet where he wants, usually his house. If we want to go out, he'll let us know if the location is bullshit. If it is, he'll stay at home.

The seventh and last child of the Fogg clan, Rodney, whom we call Rod, came with a vengeance. I thought Mama was done pushing out babies. Rod was the child who got into everything. It's something about the last child. I remember him coming home as a baby. He was so adorable, and I couldn't stop looking at him. However, I was afraid to hold him because he was so little.

As soon as he was able to move around, all hell broke loose.

He misbehaved by jumping on the bed, and even when we told him to stop, he wouldn't listen. He just laughed and ignored us. He jumped right off the bed and hit his head on the edge of a dresser. When he got up, he had a nasty hole in his head. Blood was everywhere. We all looked at each other, knowing our mother was going to fuck us up even though it wasn't our fault. We let our parents know, and we got cursed out and beat as if we'd pushed him off the bed. Rod went to the hospital to get stitches.

When they got back, we all got our asses beat again. Rod still tends to go exploring and getting himself caught in crazy situations. He has a child who looks just like him. He's still in the stage of his life when hanging out and having a great time is a priority.

My parents kept us extremely sheltered as children, so I grew up only knowing my close family, such as my grandma, aunts, uncles, and first cousins, with the exception of Great-Aunt Flordee. Sadly, I don't even know all my first cousins. I learned that my mom is the black sheep of her siblings, so we didn't hang around everyone.

My mom's brother, Lee Jr., came by a family gathering. He loves to talk shit and he scared me. He asked if I wanted to see his knife, and I shook my head. He chased me around outside with his knife. I ran into the backyard and closed the gate. What is it with my family and knives?

My uncle Wilbur was a drunk, and he wasn't ashamed of it. He always had the best time of his life when I saw him. My aunt Charity is a sweetheart, and she's also my favorite aunt. Yes, she was named after her mama. I'm not sure if that's standard, or if that's some backwoods, Alabama shit. Aunty Charity is always full of life. She moved to Texas. When she visited Rocket City, she made sure we had a good time. We did things together as a family. We'd watch movies and play board games. Her sons and I played video games, which was my favorite thing to do with them. She'd take us places in her Volvo station wagon. She used to sing,

"Cadillac car. Cadillac car. Cadillac car. Cadillac car. Kareem Abdul-Jabbar." I still don't know where this song originated from, but it was enjoyable as much as it was hilarious. Growing up, I honestly wished she was my mother.

After Grandma Charity passed, the dynamic of the entire family changed.

2

Hallelujah Day

everend Lee Mallory Sr. was my maternal grandfather. Mama said his parents, siblings, and cousins all stayed over the river. I'm assuming that meant across the bridge that was over the Tennessee River. I never asked, and I don't recall ever visiting them. Mama said they used to visit them after church on Sundays when she was little.

He had twelve siblings. They all shared the same father, but a few had different mothers. Grandpa Lee's mom died after giving birth to him. By the time my mama was born, her paternal grandparents were deceased.

Grandpa was a well-known preacher in the Rocket City area. If you were in the church realm while he lived, you knew who he was. Due to this fact, his wife and children were a reflection of him, and they needed to uphold the image of his teachings accordingly. They weren't allowed to indulge in worldly things that might tarnish the Mallory name. He made sure his children knew who God was, and he instilled knowing and loving your family into their hearts. Since he passed before I was born, I never met him or was directly influenced by his lessons. I've only heard stories from family about what a great man he was. However, my mother, Cheryl, ensured I was able to obtain my Christian experience via her teachings.

I've seen one picture of my granddad, but it was in black and white. He appeared to be extremely light-skinned with pretty eyes like my mama. He also appeared to have a fine grade of hair. He had a defined nose and chin. His top lip was very thin, and he had moles under his eye and one close to his chin. I wish I could see more pictures of him. Some of my aunts and uncles look just like him. My mom looks like him too, but she looks like Grandma Charity as well. They said he dressed really nice and was madly in love with Charity. He was always presentable unless he was working in the field.

In addition to preaching, he was a farmer. He started farming when he was a little boy. I think a lot of people farmed back in those days. It was the job assigned back then based on the caste system in America. There was so much farmland in Pond Beat County. Even while I was growing up, I saw cotton fields, corn-fields, collard green fields, horse pastures, and cow pastures. I'm sure there was more than that, but that's all I saw. Due to him working as a farmer, he kept a garden in his yard, which helped provide his own food for the family. Farming and gardening are lost skills. Grandma continued following the tradition of having a garden because she had one in her yard, mostly tomatoes. We weren't supposed to play near the garden, but the tomatoes stood out to me.

Grandpa didn't attend school. I suppose it wasn't required back then. Most boys were probably put to work outside and the girls probably tended to the inside chores, such as cooking, clean-ing, and helping care for their siblings. I couldn't imagine not going to school. It makes me wonder if all children did not attend school or just black kids. Regardless, it seemed that he did really well without having a formal education. He was loved by many, and his family turned out just fine.

My introduction to church started at a young age. I was born into church life. I hadn't even started school yet. Congregating for church started off in my family's home. I've never known us to go to any other church unless we were visiting locally or out-of-town. There was not an official, physical church building in which we attended. I don't recall if the church had a name when it first started. But I was a child, and I really didn't care about any of that back then. (To be fair, I don't care much about it now.) Every Sunday, members and visitors of the church came to our house for service. Cars filled the driveway, the street, and parts of our yard. We congregated in our den. We already had a sofa bed in there as well as a bench. We just added folding chairs when Sunday morning arrived. We also set out church fans and tambourines. Some people brought their own personalized fans, tambourines, and seat cushions. Besides the tambourines, we didn't have any instruments. All songs were sung a cappella. All members sang even though not everyone sounded the greatest. Many members were family or extended family. They came in all different shapes and sizes. Some were short and fat. Some were really tall and fat. A lot of them had Jheri curls.

My father's brother, John Fogg, and his family, which included his wife, Delia, stepchild, and step-grandchildren were members. John was tall and skinny, but Delia was the opposite. Although his brother attended church, my father never attended a single service. He wasn't a religious man. As far as I know, it never bothered my mama. I guess opposites really do attract.

My mother's colleague Bernice Crim and her family, which included her sister, Carrie Crim, and Carrie's children were also members. Bernice was really tall and big with a huge butt. She was big like Rasputia from *Norbit*. Carrie was tall and average-sized. They both had Jheri curls.

The younger kids didn't usually attend church service. We stayed out of the way until it was over, which usually lasted a few hours. That was fine with me because they were always loud. Our denomination was Apostolic Pentecostal, and we were known for having abnormally long and loud services. The other kids and I usually played outside or inside one of the bedrooms with toys or watched TV. My dad peeked in to make sure we were behaving. He'd get on to me because I was always playing with the boys instead of the girls. I'd let the girls play with my dolls while I played with my brothers and their GI Joes. We eventually went outside and played tag or hide-and-seek.

After the service was over, my siblings and I sniffed the seats to see which church members' butts stank. When we found one that smelled, we'd look up and start laughing. Jack told us which person had been sitting in that seat since he'd attended the service. Every time we saw that person again, we giggled. Looking back, it was nasty to do that, but we found it funny.

My dad, his brother, and any other men who wanted to hang out talked on the porch over beers and cigarettes. Some people stayed for dinner. Most of the women congregated in the kitchen and dining room areas. Although church was over, the kids still had to stay out of the way. We were not allowed to be in grown folks' business. Food was brought to us in the back rooms. If we needed anything additional, we had to ask one of the bigger kids to get it for us.

As I got older, I eventually had to attend church every Sunday with few exceptions. I never liked it. My daddy didn't have to attend, so I was confused as to why I had to go. I tried to get my daddy to convince my mama to let me sit out, but he lost that battle. I did not like dressing up. I felt like I had on too many clothes. It wasn't comfortable. It usually consisted of a slip, dress, stockings or bobby socks, and some tight-ass shoes that always made my feet hurt. I looked like I was ready to start tap dancing in those shoes.

My mom did my hair, and it hurt while she combed and brushed it. Tears formed in my eyes, and she told me to be still. She put a ton of bows or barrettes in it. Everyone said I was so cute, but I felt overwhelmed. She had me looking like Little Magic from *In Living Color*. Give me my pajamas or jeans and a T-shirt with my tennis shoes any day.

My mother's preaching usually lasted a long time. She preached like the men when they were huffing and puffing intentionally for extra effect. It's not necessary to do that long gasp for breath at the end of every sentence. If you're that tired, sit down and take a break. All that extra is uncalled for—but the congregation loved it.

On top of providing the message, she called people out for what they were doing wrong, including regularly missing church, not paying tithes, doing worldly things, among other issues. It seemed some people were targeted. I wondered if she created her sermons based on the church members' life experiences. For example, if she knew one of the members went to a concert, she revolved her sermon around that. She requested that everyone open their bibles to the scripture about lusting for flesh. Once we all got to that chapter and verse, she requested Sister Bernice to read it.

After reading it, Mama said, "Thank you. If you love the Lord, you don't do things to disobey his word. Sister Crim, it was brought to my attention that you attended an Al Green concert, and you lusted over his physical appearance and danced in a provocative way to his music. That is not of God. 'I'm Still in Love with You' is not God-like."

I was embarrassed for her. Everyone got really quiet. The rest of the sermon stayed focused on the scripture, but everyone knew it was because of Ms. Crim going to the concert. She talked about people who didn't pay their tithes—but, she said, she heard they were at the mall buying new clothes and shoes. She picked on people who didn't show up for service, because she'd heard they were out late the previous night. It was a total shit show. If you didn't abide by the rules, you were called out.

Not only did she call people out during the sermon, she called them out when it was time for her to prophesy. The Lord touched her spirit to tell someone what was about to happen and what they needed to do to get in line to prevent bad things from occurring. Those things ranged from what type of job to get, who to date, how to come up with money, how to stop partying, how to pay your tithes, how to never miss services, among other things. Sometimes she laid hands on people while prophesying, and they would catch the Holy Spirit. They'd start shouting and speaking in tongues. The usher, which was usually anybody close who wanted to help, had to calm them down. If it was a lady, they usually passed out on the floor. The usher would lay a blanket across them so you wouldn't see their undergarments. Even though people passed out, the service continued on. She just moved right on to the next person.

Testimony service was an entirely different beast. It lasted forever because everyone had a testimony. My mother encouraged everyone to share what they were thankful for because everyone had to be thankful for something.

It started with us saying, "Rising and giving honor to God who is the head of my life." If you didn't begin with that, you weren't taught by Pastor Fogg. If I couldn't think of anything I was thankful for, I had to say I was thankful for God waking me up this morning and watching over me last night. Just imagine going through this with at least twenty members. Some people felt the need to tell their life stories. They always felt like they had to outdo each other. It's like they were in a competition to make my mama proud of them.

"Rising and giving honor to God," Ms. Bernice Crim would say, "who is the head of my life. He woke me up this morning and watched over me last night. Pastor helped me get a car this past weekend. She negotiated with the salesman, and we got the car below the asking price. Thank you, Jesus!"

Here was her sister trying to outdo her. Carrie Crim followed up with, "Praise the Lord, saints! I can't hear y'all. Praise the Lord, saints! Rising and giving honor to the Almighty God, who is the head of all our lives. He watched over us last night, and he woke us up ever so gracefully this morning. Let me tell you what the pastor has done for me. She too helped me get a nice automobile. Not only did we get the car under the asking price, we also got a great interest rate. She also helped me get into a nice house not too far from where she stays. That way it won't be a burden for me to make it to church on time. Amen."

Bernice then said, "Recap! Y'all know I've been in my house for three months, which the pastor helped me obtain. Not only did she help me get my house, she went furniture shopping with me. We work together at the salon, so we spend a lot of time together. We were in that store for hours until God spoke to her to let me know the exact furniture that I needed to purchase. We were able to get it at a great price. Amen! Glory! Hallelujah! Eee-bah-bah-shun-dah!"

It was a total mess. Let's not forget my aunt Delia, John Fogg's wife, who had to take her sweet time with everything. "Praise the Lord, everybody. Rise and giving honor to God, who is the head of my life. He's the reason I live and breathe. I thank him for my husband. I thank him for my daughter. I thank him for my grand-kids. I thank him for this church. I thank him for everybody in this church. I thank him for allowing me to pay my bills. I thank him for putting food on the table. He didn't have to do it, but he did. Last but certainly not least, I thank him for my pastor. Amen! Amen! Amen!"

When someone actually said something profound, it was al-ways followed by shouting or speaking in tongues, which freaked me out the first time I saw it happen. That just added more time to the service. They also had to outdo each other when shouting and speaking in tongues. It seemed like they wanted to see who could go the longest as well as who had the best dance.

One service, Delia started shouting and speaking in tongues. She got excited and ran right out of the door into the street. Now that was theatrical. I felt like I was just sitting there wasting time. I was trying not to lose my mind and hoping the Holy Ghost didn't get me. Most of us kids just laughed and talked about people when the antics started. Some of us got caught, and we were told to be quiet. If we kept acting up, we got dirty looks. We all knew that meant we'd get our asses beat later, so we'd shut the fuck up. Carrie's son was a rebel, so he kept going. He eventually got put out of the service. He peeked back into the room, got caught, and got the evil eye from his mama and auntie.

As a leader in the church, Mama was always helping people. Sometimes I felt like she helped them more than she helped her own kids. It seemed like she was helping people when she didn't even have the means to do so. A song we sang in church said the more you give, the more you get back. She believed in those lyrics. She assisted Bernice and her sister with getting vehicles and housing. She loaned money to many church members. She allowed many people to stay over for dinner. She gave away toys we didn't play with and clothes we didn't wear to people in need. Sometimes, she even bought them new clothes. When she got new furniture, she gave away our old furniture to members. She let people buy her old cars from her when she got new ones.

Giving was never-ending. A visiting churchgoer, Tobe Campbell, lived with us for a few years. We already had nine people living in a three-bedroom house. We didn't need anyone else adding to the crowded situation. This was one of those times when I felt like we didn't have the means. Why couldn't he stay with Bernice? She had no husband nor any children.

To make room for Tobe, Jack had to share the den with him.

I'm sure that was a huge inconvenience. Jack was a teenager, so I'm sure he was probably masturbating by then. The washroom was only accessible through the den, so now he really had no privacy with Tobe moving in. As a result, our cousins joked with Jack, stating Tobe was his daddy. He got really mad. He already had to sacrifice the den for church on Sundays, and now he had to share it full time with a stranger.

Jack said Tobe used to fart in his sleep, and he snored really loud. Mama should've just helped him find housing, as she did with the Crim sisters. In addition to him farting, Tobe took shits that made half the house stink. I don't know what was in his system, but he needed it cleansed. He did help Mama around the house when it came to painting. He eventually taught her how to paint.

As time went on we warmed up to him, and he became just like family. He participated in meals, birthdays, and holidays. His mom and a few of his siblings visited our church occasionally. They would also stay for dinner. On those days, Mama didn't make us attend church because it was too crowded. She did his mom's and sister's hair in the kitchen every so often, and we were never allowed in there. A child needs to stay in a child's place. That was what we were told. Stay out of grown people's business.

As time moved on, the dynamic of the church began to evolve. We rotated locations between our house and Uncle John's house. This helped relieve Jack and Tobe of rearranging their belongings every Sunday to prepare for church. I know they were happy. They didn't have to let in the sofa bed unless they wanted to.

This was when I realized the church had a name. During one church service, we all received bibles. Someone donated new bibles to our congregation. On the outside, it was pretty—black leather with gold lettering. The pages were outlined in red, so from the outside with the book closed, it was all red between the leather cover. On the inside cover was a space to write your name and the name of the church. The new-book smell was amazing. I flipped through the pages and inhaled. All the kids looked around at each other not knowing what we were supposed to write. We didn't recall Mama ever saying the name of the church. We felt like we were in trouble because we didn't know. However, even some of the adults looked puzzled. That made us feel a little better. We were told to write our names and the following: Real Spiritual House of Salvation. It's sad that I didn't know the name of the church, but as I indicated, most of us kids really didn't care. We went to church because we were forced to. We didn't pay attention to service most of the time. It was good to know the church had a name, but I still didn't care much because I didn't want to go.

I looked around Uncle John's living room, where we congregated. It was not as big and accommodating as our den. It was extra crowded. We were basically stacked on top of one another. Because of this, the kids did not have to attend service at his house. I was overjoyed. We played in his huge backyard. Eventually, we stopped having service at any of the houses.

After working at different beauty salons across the city, my mother eventually built her own. I was so happy for her. She could stop doing people's hair in the house. We could get our kitchen back full time, which gave us the opportunity to get our own food versus being told to stay out of grown folks' business.

Being the giving woman she is, my mother offered Bernice an opportunity to rent a booth in her salon. Bernice gladly accepted. The salon also provided a new place to congregate for church. Tobe and Jack got the den back full time. No one had to worry about getting their house in order to prepare for service. It was a win for everyone. Years later, Mama eventually had a church built not far from her salon, which freed up the beauty salon to be used solely as a beauty salon. Look at God!

3

Elementary School

I skipped kindergarten. It wasn't required when I was a child. I suppose it's like pre-k is today. It wasn't mandatory, but it was good to get your child acclimated to a learning environment around other children. I was terrified of the thought of going to school. I didn't want to acclimate to a damn thing. I was fine staying where I had been all these years, at home with my family. I think my mother decided to let me stay home because I cried over the thought of leaving the house to be with strangers. I'm so glad she felt my pain.

I was always up under my siblings, so I didn't know how to function without family. I might as well had gone to school because my mother sometimes left me at home with no supervision. How the hell do you leave a five-year-old child solo? It probably would've been better to be scared around strangers than to be scared at home by my lonesome. I once watched *A Nightmare on Elm Street*. Who the hell leaves her child in front of the TV watching horror movies? What happened to shows like *Sesame Street*? She could've left the TV on cartoons, soap operas, the news, anything other than horror flicks. I guess she was in a hurry and didn't bother to see what was on TV before she left. I was terrified, but my dumb ass still watched the whole movie as if I couldn't look away, turn the TV off, change the channel, or go into another room. It's like it was asking me to watch it, and I told it I would.

After finishing the movie, all I learned was that I was not supposed to fall asleep, or Freddy would get me. I waited in that bedroom staring out of the window for Shawn to walk home from school. The school was right up the street, but it seemed like it took forever for him to get home. Staring out the window into daylight thinking about him getting home helped calm my nerves. I refused to be in the dark, and I refused to fall asleep. Let that natural light shine through the window. As time passed, I finally saw him walking in the street. As he got closer to the house, I ran from the bedroom to the front door to meet him with a big hug. You'd think I'd be scared to watch horror movies now, but I actually love them. I turned my childhood trauma into a hobby.

After a year passed, it was time for me to go to school. There was no crying my way out of it this time even though I still tried. My mother made sure I went to school. I don't blame her. I suppose the alternative would have been for her to let me stay home, but then she could go to jail. She woke me up early, got me dressed, did my hair, fed me, and sent me on my way.

I started first grade at age six. The school mascot was an owl, but I didn't give a hoot about being there. Once again, I was terrified, but I suppose it was better than being left home alone. I had never been around kids outside my home without other family being around. Shawn was at the school with me, but he was three grades ahead. He had his own friends, and he was familiar with the school. He didn't want to be bothered with me. Mama had Shawn walk me to my class. He took me to my teacher and then left.

I cried like a baby when he left to go to his own classroom. I sat there trying to calm down, but it took a while. I eventually stopped crying and realized I had to pee.

I told the teacher I needed to pee, and she replied, "It's not breaktime. You can go use the restroom during breaktime."

I was not used to taking instructions from strangers, but I was compelled to follow the rules. I held it as long as I could. Breaktime didn't come fast enough, so I peed myself. I was so embarrassed and didn't say anything. I just started crying. I sat there pissy for the rest of the school day.

My mother was furious when I got home. She asked me why I peed on myself, and I told her. She said, "If you ever have to go to the bathroom, just go. I don't care what anybody tells you. They can deal with me. Got my car smelling like piss."

She had a talk with the teacher. The teacher actually came to our house since it was right down the street. My mother let me sit outside with them, so I could listen to their conversation.

The teacher lied and said, "I never said she couldn't go to the restroom. She never asked if she could go."

My mother asked me, "Is that what happened?"

I shook my head.

She told me to go into the house. I don't know how the rest of the conversation went, but I was good to go to the restroom from then on regardless of what anyone told me. The teacher never bothered me again.

The rest of my years in elementary school were interesting. The first time I noticed boys in a different light was in second grade. I wouldn't say I was boy crazy, but one of them grabbed my attention. My first crush was Sylvester. He seemed extremely tall, but I think I was extremely short for my age. We played with each other on the playground during recess. My way of flirting with him was picking with him to get him riled up. I pushed him and ran, threw rocks at him, stuck my tongue out at him, and many other childish things. If any of those actions occurred, he immediately chased me. I suppose he was my Sylvester, and I was his Tweety. After he caught me, he looked at me and smiled. I smiled back and then ran again. I bossed him around a lot. I made him push me on the swings. I made him get on the see-saw with me. We played house in the jungle gym, and I fussed at him the way I saw my mama fuss at my daddy when she was mad at him.

Other than Sylvester, there wasn't anyone else I gave that much attention to. There was a guy in my class named Jason who asked to borrow my crayons. We had to color for an assignment, and I guess his parents didn't buy him any. I let him borrow my crayons, and he never gave them back. Instead of asking for them back at the end of the assignment, I went off on him. I guess I felt I shouldn't have to ask for my own shit back. I started cussing him out. Outside of hearing bad words from my parents and TV, Jack taught me profanity. My teacher told me to calm down, and I did as soon as I got my crayons back. Jason and I had to apologize to each other.

My classroom outburst led to the many sessions I had with the guidance counselor due to my misbehaving. We talked about my behavior while playing Hi-Ho! Cherry-O! She asked if I knew why I was in her office. She asked why I did what I did. She also asked if I knew it was wrong. I always answered while crying, but I was really heavily focused on playing the game. She was focused on my behavior, and I was focused on collecting all my cherries. I did not want to lose.

In addition to recess, PE was the bomb. It was simple fun, and we didn't focus on being extremely competitive, even though being competitive is part of any sport or game. My favorite PE teacher was Coach Miller. She introduced me to synchronized dancing, and I loved dancing from then on out. We learned a dance to a song called "Elvira" by the Oak Ridge Boys. The dance was performed while being seated on the gym floor. The highlight for me was when we scooted up on our butts and imitated spinning a lasso in the air during the part where they sang, "Giddy up, oom poppa, oom poppa, mow mow! Hi-ho Silver, away!" It made me so happy to be on my imaginary horse dancing to this song. This was definitely some country-ass 'Bama shit.

We also played a game called Pass the Bean Bag, and it had a song to it as well. Besides dancing, we had races on scooters that had handles on their sides and four wheels. We held the handles and used our feet and leg strength to complete laps. We scooted from the starting line on one end of the gym, around a cone at the opposite end, and back to the starting line. Whether I won or lost, I just liked being on the scooter.

We played Red Rover, and I didn't mind when they "called me right over." I tried to destroy people's arms to get through. When it was time for someone to break through, I held my partner's arm extra tight to ensure that person didn't pass.

Dodgeball was also interesting. The sound of that ball hitting me will forever ring in my head. The sounds of kids screaming while running around was hilarious. I never wanted to get hit, but I loved trying to hit someone with the ball.

I also enjoyed other simple activities, such as jumping rope and playing with hula hoops. I never fully got the hang of keeping the hula hoop up. If I couldn't keep it around my waist, then I surely couldn't put it around my neck. Lastly, we had relay races on the track. This was probably one of the most competitive games as a team. You had to heavily depend on your teammates to ensure you all finished your laps first. One time, I was waiting to be passed the baton; I grabbed it and took off running. A few seconds later, I fell. I got back up and fell again. I tried once more, and I fell again. I hobbled all the way to my teammate to pass the baton, and I left the track. I don't know what happened because I wasn't hurt. It was just one of those clumsy days, much like the days when we learned how to jump hurdles. Let's just say I fell a lot or knocked a lot of them down and kept moving.

We had activities at the school as a whole, which allowed families to attend. Andy would be the one to always tag along with me because my parents were always busy. He graduated high school after I finished first grade, and he immediately took on more responsibilities to help take care of me and my siblings.

Kite Day was a family event. All the kids had to bring a kite from home. My parents were usually cheap when it came to buying things, so I was surprised when they actually bought me a nice kite. My dad got me a Barbie kite even though I wanted a GI Joe kite like Shawn's. There was something so soothing and freeing about flying a kite. Just watching the way it floated in air was liberating. I wanted to be like that kite, to float around in the wind among my other kite friends with no worries or cares. I enjoyed seeing the beauty in the designs the students brought. It was nice seeing them flying simultaneously, but getting the kites to fly was a chore. Andy and Coach Miller walked me through running at full speed and releasing the line slowly to get it to fly. I learned to wait for the perfect breeze. If not, my kite dragged on the ground as I ran. It took several attempts, but I eventually got the hang of it.

Besides Kite Day, we had Field Day. There were different stations set up for food, candy, and games. It was like a mini-carnival. My parents gave me money to spend, and Andy had to make sure I spent it wisely. We had activities, such as ring toss, horseshoes, potato sack races, and many more. My favorite was the sack race. It was funny to try winning a race by hopping around in a sack. Field Day was a day made to eat junk, have fun, and win prizes.

School wasn't always fun and games. My first experience with being bullied was around third grade. I don't even know why it happened because I never bothered the girl. I truly believe hurt people hurt people. Some were taught to hurt people just because they're different. This girl just seemed to not like me. I know my mother dressed me differently from most of the kids. I was extremely well dressed, like I was going to church. If not church, then it looked like I was always ready for picture day. My attire consisted of a dress, dress shoes, and thick, Medicaid-prescribed glasses. Yes, I was blind as a bat. I got glasses in second grade. We were on Medicaid, so I had to get the glasses that fell into the program. The frames were thick, and the lenses were just as thick. Coke-bottle thick lenses. Ugh! If a coat was needed, I had a trench coat. Mind you, I grew up in an urban neighborhood. No one in my neighborhood wore this shit. The white kids at the school didn't even dress this formally. I also had a briefcase instead of a book bag.

One day after school, this girl called me a nerd and punched me in the stomach. I cried like a baby. I didn't even know what nerd meant. I was eight years old. My neighbor, who lived down the street from us saw the incident. He looked after me until my mom arrived to pick me up.

Through my pain and tears, I looked up at him and asked, "What's a nerd?"

He said, "Someone who's really smart. Don't ever change."

The bully is now a servant of the Lord. Go figure!

I was made fun of because of my last name. You don't know how odd your last name is until people make fun of it. Instead of Fogg, they called me any type of weather, such as rain and snow. I was called Foggy Bottom. Where do people come up with this kind of stuff? Teachers added an s to my last name. I never understood that. I don't know if they were trying to make a subtle joke, or if they were just really ignorant. I suppose that was their way of getting in a jab. Some people spelled it with just one g. I'm thinking that was also a jab. Getting bullied by teachers and students was no fun. It seemed like I just couldn't win.

As the years went by, I was able to persuade my dad to convince my mom to let me dress differently, so I'd quit getting bullied. My mom had to approve everything. Thankfully, it worked out. My mother was pissed, so she let my dad do my school shopping. I was able to wear jeans, T-shirts, and tennis shoes. I started wearing my hair in a simple ponytail instead of having all those bows and barrettes. I was able to get a regular bookbag. I had a jacket and a regular coat. Like Patti LaBelle said, "I got a new attitude." However, my glasses were still thick, and I still got picked on. Because of this, I became a problem child. I was still smart and had excellent grades. I was always on the honor roll. I just stayed in trouble. I think it was because I felt like I had something to prove. I was fed up with being bullied and called a nerd. I'd cuss kids out who picked with me. I cracked jokes on them. Whenever people talked about me, I was quick to respond, "Your mama," "Your daddy," or "Your greasy granny with the holes in her panties." Thanks, older brothers, for teaching me how to roast.

Speaking of older brothers, Jack remixed "Have You Seen Her" by MC Hammer into a song about a menstrual cycle. My dumb ass wrote it down, took it to school, and got caught passing it around. That led to a phone call home to my mother, and I got my ass beat.

I don't recall every bad thing I did, but I was always getting ass whippings. It seemed like every other day I was bending over my parents' bed to get a beating. My mother put on gloves to beat our asses so she wouldn't hurt her hands. One time, she came to the school and threatened to beat my ass in front of the entire class. She was tired of me getting into trouble. Apparently, it didn't matter because I still played Hi-Ho! Cherry-O! during the majority of my elementary school years. One time I got in trouble, and my mother told me she was going to beat my ass. She was busy for the rest of the day, so I figured I'd get a beating the following day. However, I was awakened out of my sleep by belt lashes. I'm sure this is now considered child abuse.

In fifth grade, we all had to take a health class. When it was time to take this class, which was a one-time session versus all year, the boys and the girls were split up in different rooms. I honestly don't know what the boys talked about, but the girls talked about menstrual cycles. I knew it had to do with bleeding because of the song Jack told me about, but I honestly had no idea every girl was going to have a period. I was devastated. I didn't want to bleed out of my TT. That's what my mom always called it, but I later learned it's a vagina. I don't know if TT is common, or if that's just a term that was used in my family to prevent us from sounding too grown.

We watched a short video about becoming a woman. The health instructor sent us home with a pamphlet. When I got home, I gave it to my mom. She read it, and she gave me "the talk" about getting my period. She then gave me a talk about boys and how they will try to put their TT in my TT. I was puzzled, wondering how that worked, but I kept my mouth closed. She told me that's how you get a baby, and I shouldn't do anything like that until I was grown and married.

"Do you understand me?" Mama asked.

"Yes, ma'am," I replied.

The following weekend we went shopping for panty liners and pads. When we got home, she showed me how to use them, so I'd be ready. She told me to keep a couple in my bookbag just in case. Toward the end of the school year, a classmate got her period, and it was noticeable. You saw blood on her pants and in her seat. All the girls in the class knew what was going on, but the boys seemed clueless. One boy thought someone put a tack in her seat as a prank that went horribly wrong.

She got escorted to the clinic, and she went home. That incident made me nervous. That could have been me. Most of the girls were gossiping, but I continued to do my work. That afternoon I told my mom what happened to the girl.

Three days before the last day of school, I got my period. It just came out of nowhere. I wasn't even feeling bad. I asked to be excused to go to the restroom. As I got out of my chair, I grabbed my jacket from the back of the chair and wrapped it around my waist. I checked the seat to make sure I didn't leave any evidence. I didn't see anything. I grabbed my bookbag and went to the clinic. I already had everything I needed in my bag. I changed my panties and applied my pad. My jeans were slightly spotted. I waited for my mom to pick me up. I was scared she'd beat my ass because I wasn't wearing the panty liners as she told me, and I'd spotted my jeans.

While I waited for her to show up, the cramping finally started. She arrived, and I was prepared for her to fuss at me. Instead, she consoled me, and I didn't go back to school for the rest of that school year. I continued to wonder what the boys could have talked about in their class. Looking back, it was probably about wet dreams. I don't think they were teaching them about condoms that early. I guess I'll never know.

4

Onward to Middle School

fter summer vacation, it would be time for me to attend middle school. The family went to Six Flags over Georgia to enjoy our break from school. We all traveled tightly in the family van, which was an old Ford Econoline named Bessie. I don't know who gave the van that name. I always felt like we were in the Mystery Machine, and Shawn's old dog face was Scooby. It had two seats up front, two seats in the middle, and a long seat in the back. There was a bar-style table in front of the long backseat. Except for the two front passenger windows, all other passenger windows had wooden blinds.

My parents sat in the two front seats. Andy and Jack sat in the two middle seats. The rest of us had to figure out where the hell we were going to sit in the back. It was a tight squeeze, but we made it work. We'd occasionally get bored or tired of being shoulder to shoulder, so we'd walk around the back area. Mama had control over what we listened to, and it was always gospel. My nerves got so worked. I'd get tired of listening to her music. Jack had a Walkman, so I occasionally got his headphones to listen to his music, which was usually a mix of rap and R&B.

When Mama wasn't playing gospel, she listened to the CB radio. We were all excited to take this road trip, but no one wanted to listen to anything my mother chose. My parents didn't like to make stops unless they were stopping for food or to go to the restroom. I had to use the restroom, but no one else did, so I was told to hold it. It's funny how my mama told me I can go to the bathroom when I needed to, but they wouldn't stop. I should've peed on the van's carpet. I got to the point where I couldn't hold it any longer. There was a bucket in the van, and my dad told me to pee in the bucket. I was embarrassed because I didn't want to pee in front of everybody. However, I couldn't hold it. My mom told my brothers not to look. For the rest of the ride, my brothers called me Etta Pee Bucket.

Right before we got to Six Flags, we pulled to the side of the road to dump the bucket. When we finally arrived in Six Flags' parking lot, Mama gave her long speech about us not asking for shit as well as us not running off from each other. We all nodded to let her know we understood the rules.

We walked from the parking lot to the line to purchase tickets. My mom saw a sign stating children ages five and younger get in the park for free. She looked at Rod and said, "When we get to the gate, if they ask you how old you are, you tell them you're five." He nodded.

We made it to the gate agent, who asked how many tickets, and my mother told him nine. He went through each person, and my mom gave the age of everyone as he asked.

When the agent got to Rod, she said, "He's five."

Rod replied, "Uh-uh! I'm six."

The look on her face was priceless. It could've burned a hole through Rod's chest.

She responded to the agent, "Oh that's right! He just had a

birthday." She had to pay for a child's ticket instead of him getting in free. Once we got our tickets and walked through the gate, she snatched him up as soon as she got the chance.

Mom planned our route through the park. She advised all water rides must come first, so we'd be dry by the time we left. So we rode the two water rides, which were the river ride and the log ride. We got soaked. Afterward, we walked around the park riding rides in the order they came. On this trip, I learned that amusement parks are not for me. I rode the swings, which seemed bearable. However, I learned I have an issue with riding anything that goes around in circles. I was extremely nauseated, and I felt like I was going to fall as soon as I got off of the ride. To not feel embarrassed, I told my parents I could continue on because my brothers kept calling me a wuss. I got on my last ride for that trip. It was a roller coaster. I should've just sat back with my parents, who didn't ride anything at all. I threw up all over myself. It even got inside my shoes, and when we got to the hotel, they had the entire room stinking. I earned the nickname of Stinky Feet that evening. We headed back to Alabama the following morning.

The rest of my summer was pretty chill. Jack and Shawn introduced me to BET and MTV. It was the early 1990s, and the videos they showed had a whole lot of booty shaking. I totally enjoyed watching the dances. This was different from the dances I learned in PE. However, I decided I wanted to learn these booty-shaking moves too. "Da Butt" was one of my favorites. When I got that notion, I put my backfield in motion. I may not have had any titties to save my life, but my cheeks made up for what I lacked up top. I would shake my thang and "Push It" with Salt-N-Pepa. Outside of shaking it like a salt shaker, I played video games, watched cartoons, and hung out with kids in the neighborhood. We were all dreading going back to school.

Summer was officially over, and I transitioned from being an owl to a bulldog. These middle school years were when I was coming into myself. I was growing into a teenager. The school was no longer right down the street from my house. However, it was still within walking distance. I was introduced to school lockers. We didn't have these in elementary school. We had a cubby drawer, and it was not locked. Everyone had access to each other's cubby drawer. I now had to learn how to use a combination lock. It took me a few tries to get it right, but I eventually did. I was also used to being in one class all day long. Now we had pods. The pod had approximately four different classes in them, but they were separated by partitions. You could see the other students in the other classes if you sat near the back row, and you could also hear them, which was a bit distracting. Homeroom was the first class of the day. It was basically where you were accounted for and learned anything needed about the school to include listening to announcements. Since there was not really any work to do, this was where students cut up and had a great time. We were usually still trying to wake up. After homeroom, we attended our normal classes. The only classes held outside of the pods were electives and PE.

There were a lot of familiar faces as well as new ones. For the first time, I was able to go to school with a couple of my first cousins on my mom's side. They were Lee Mallory Jr.'s daughters, and they had long, pretty hair. We always spoke when we saw each other, but we didn't have any classes together. One was in the same grade as me, and the other was a grade under me.

I became good friends with a guy named Earl. He told me that he lived around the street from me. When I played in the neighborhood, it was always with people who lived on the same street. My parents didn't let me go too far, so I knew nothing of him before middle school. He told me he went to the same elementary school as me, but I don't recall seeing him there. He was a nerd with big glasses, just like me. He enjoyed playing video games, and I told him I played quite often. He told me he had all kinds of fun things to do at his house and suggested I come over one day. I told him I'd run it by my mom, and I'd let him know. For the time being, we only got acquainted at school.

As time went on, I became popular for a couple of reasons. For one, I was extremely intelligent. My classmates saw what type of grades I received. They wanted to cheat off of my paper or pay me to do their homework. I was lazy, so I was not about to do anyone's homework. I may have been a nerd, but my attitude was not of a nerd. I'd tell them they could pay me to copy off my paper. The other reason for my popularity was that the boys were drawn to the size of my ass. It was a blessing and a curse. During lunch, PE, and after school I sang and danced. It's just what I loved doing. My parents were still cheap, so I couldn't join the band, dance team, or cheerleading squad, so I danced on my own whenever I got the opportunity. The boys would rap, beatbox, and make beats on the table. I'd be right there with them, dancing and singing. There were some girls who would have a great time with us while other girls hated the fact that I was getting attention from the guys. But I was there for fun and was in my own world. Those girls still thought otherwise. I considered them the mean girls. They were the popular girls who were extremely pretty. They all had breasts. I only wore a bra because of PE guidelines. I didn't really need one.

They talked about me across the room as if I couldn't hear them. One girl said, "The only thing shaking is her butt because she doesn't have anything else."

I stopped dancing and singing and said, "I'm shaped like ya ugly mammy."

This led to us fussing and cussing each other out.

She pinned me down on the lunchroom table and whispered in my ear, "Bitch, I'm not trying to fight you, but you need to quit hogging all the attention. I could easily beat your ass." She was probably right.

A teacher separated us, and we were sent to detention.

Boys were really not heavy on my mind. I noticed them, but they were not a priority for me. Since the popular girls tried to keep me away from hanging with the guys, I decided to try to date one. Those girls won't play me like that. Brent was one of the boys who really liked me, and he was somewhat popular. He walked home from school, and occasionally, I did too. Sometimes, we'd walk together as a group with other students. He flirted with me and kissed me. I didn't know anything about boys, so I just let him. I just knew he wasn't putting his TT in my TT. He was cute, but he wasn't a crush of mine. He was a little rough around the edges. I'm assuming he didn't stay too far from where I lived because he was always walking down my street. If he saw me outside, he made sure to stop to speak from the end of the street.

Little did he know I was interested in others. I did shoot my shot with two popular guys, but I got shot down. There was a guy named Glenn who I thought was cute, but I never let him know. I didn't want to get shot down again. He walked home in a separate group from mine. We'd speak to each other across groups. That's how a lot of us actually communicated versus forming a bigger group. I never saw any interest from him based on our conversations. I then came to the realization that I was a big nerd who would always be placed in the friend zone by people I was interested in. They only used me for entertainment or my knowledge. That's what I got for trying to date someone to make the popular girls jealous.

Physical education in middle school was totally different from PE in elementary school. It was a love/hate class for me. I only wanted to play when I felt like it. I enjoyed playing football because I played with my brothers. However, the girls weren't allowed to do that.

I hated boundary ball, which was an upgraded version of dodgeball with a bigger ball. That ball was huge. I felt like the popular girls were all targeting me. They lit my ass up. There was one boundary ball game when I actually caught the ball thrown by one of the mean girls. Everyone was surprised I caught it, and the crowd went wild. I threw the ball right back at that bitch. It hit her, and she didn't catch it. Off to the sidelines with that peasant.

I enjoyed ping pong. I also enjoyed playing basketball in the neighborhood but not in PE. It's easier to play things with people who genuinely like you versus people that don't even want to pick you for their team. One day, I wanted to sit out during basketball, and Coach Jheri Curl made me play. She said I'd get a fail for participation if I didn't. Well, it resulted in me hurting myself. I was guarding one of the girls who was actually on the basketball team. She was dribbling the ball, and I was in front of her with my arms out, making sure she didn't pass me. She did a mean crossover and shook the hell out of me. I tried to turn back quickly to make sure she didn't get away, and it was all downhill from there. I was in excruciating pain. I knew something twisted due to the way I turned. I could barely walk.

My classmate had to carry me to the nurse's office. My mother picked me up from school. I told her what happened and how bad I felt. She told me I'd be fine and I should just sleep it off. After crying day and night, we went to the hospital the next day. The pain was caused by a cracked knee. I had my first surgery and was in a cast for months. I blamed Coach Jheri. Had I known anything about suing people at the time, I would have gotten paid.

Despite my struggles in PE, there was one thing I really liked about it that I probably shouldn't have. It happened at the beginning and end of the class. It was dressing out. I was ashamed to look at the other girls, but it excited me so much. My breasts were so much smaller compared to most of my classmates', so my curiosity compelled me to look. The amount of time that I stared didn't seem right. I felt like this wasn't normal. I had never seen females getting naked in person. I watched music videos of half-naked women with their asses and titties hanging out, but it never did anything to me like my locker room experience. I tried to suppress the urges to look, but I felt as if I couldn't help myself. I was drawn to them. Some girls had really pretty bras and panties. I wore underwear that had the days of the week on them, and my training bra was basic.

Some of the girls actually got completely naked and showered. My entire body got hot the first time I saw one of my classmates naked. I bit my lip and clenched my thighs together really tight. Her breasts were perfect. My whole body tingled. From that day forward, I knew I'd change in and out really fast, and I'd never take a shower. Some of the girls talked about me because I didn't shower. They told everyone that I stank, and I wasn't clean. Wearing my cast saved me from the locker room for several months.

Once my cast was removed, I was back to my normal self. I finally asked my mom if I could hang out with Earl and his sister. I figured adding the sister part would help with her decision. My dad knew exactly who the family was because he worked with their dad. He also told my mom that her brothers went to church with their family. My mother advised me I could go.

His house was amazing. He had lots of video games and tabletop games. They had a bookshelf with an encyclopedia set as well as other books. His mom cooked and offered snacks. She introduced me to seafood I'd never heard of before. We didn't have any of this shit at our house with the exception of video games. We had a swing set in the backyard that lifted out of the ground if you swung too hard. We had a basketball goal in the middle of a dirt patch.

My new routine was to go to his house after school. We'd get our homework done first and then hang out doing random activities. It usually consisted of playing sports or video games. I didn't mind playing basketball with them because I was more comfortable. They knew my strengths and weaknesses, and they didn't mind coaching me. I was a great shot 85 percent of the time, but I couldn't dribble to save my life. It was a mix of guys and girls playing sports. We also played football in their backyard. I loved to tackle people, and I was always tough to knock down. My brothers taught me well. They had tennis rackets and tennis balls, so we'd go play at the park. We'd play volleyball and badminton in their backyard. They had all the fun stuff. It was like my second home.

When we weren't playing sports or games, they went to the park to fool around. I didn't know anything about sex, and the thought of it made me uncomfortable, so I usually stayed behind.

On one occasion I went with Earl to his girlfriend's house. She didn't go to school with us, but they went to the same church. She stayed a little ways from us, so we rode our bikes. I was just expecting to be there while they did whatever they do. They were on the couch kissing, and I sat on the loveseat waiting for them to finish. She stopped kissing him and came over to me. She straddled me on the seat. She then started kissing me. I was in awe, but my instincts kicked in to respond.

We kissed and felt each other on the loveseat in front of him for at least two minutes. It was my first experience really kissing a girl. I'm not talking a peck on the lips. I'm talking about wet tongue kissing. Our tongues locked while I felt her humongous ass. My nipples got hard, and my pussy throbbed and got wet. My whole body was hot. I was nervous and didn't want to go any further. After all, it was my friend's girlfriend, and I was a virgin. I didn't know what the fuck to do.

I pulled back from her, and she got up. I told Earl I was ready to go. We left. For some reason, he didn't get upset. I felt awkward. The bike ride home was silent. As soon as I sat on the bike seat, I felt a tingling sensation. I was still turned on. I wanted to rub my pussy up and down the seat. Earl and I didn't say much to each other the entire ride. It made me wonder if this was what they did at the park. Did they share girls? Did they all fuck each other?

There was one thing that I did know. I learned how to masturbate that night.

Weirdly, the situation was never talked about again. Earl and I continued hanging out as if nothing ever happened, but I wasn't okay with that. If I was this bothered, he should also be this bothered.

One day I was at his house, and we were alone. His parents had left to pick up his sister from volleyball practice. We played video games for most of the afternoon. When his parents left, he turned off the video game, and we started watching *Power Rangers*. I wondered if he thought I liked girls. I wondered if he told anyone about the incident. I wondered if his girlfriend told anyone. I felt like I had something to prove. After all, she came on to me.

Instead of simply having a legitimate conversation to express how I felt, I sparked up a different type of conversation. I decided to make up a lie to make myself feel better. I told him I sucked dick. He said I was lying. I told him I wasn't, and I wanted to suck his dick.

He sat in the chair across from me. I got up from my chair, walked to him, and dropped to my knees. I placed my hands on his thighs. I looked up out the window behind him through the slightly opened blinds. His parents had pulled into the driveway.

We both had a look of disappointment on our faces. I hurried back to my chair before they got into the house. Although we didn't get anywhere, I hoped that made him understand I was attracted to guys.

5

High School Bound

The summer before high school was a little sad. Earl was moving to a neighboring city, so I'd no longer have easy access to my best friend. We wouldn't be in the same neighborhood, nor would we be going to the same school. In the back of my mind, I wondered if his parents saw me through the cracked blinds preparing to give their son head, but I don't think there's any way they could have noticed.

We all went to a local amusement park as a farewell party and to celebrate our birthdays. Earl, his sister, my brother Marc, and I all had August birthdays. Leos are the greatest. We enjoyed riding go-karts and playing arcade games and miniature golf. I really suck at mini golf, but it was still fun. There was plenty of food, cake, and entertainment.

A few days later they were moved into their new home. Once they got settled, I was invited over. That gave me reassurance that they didn't see what I was trying to do to their son. I suppose they just wanted Earl to go to a better school. They moved to a predominantly white neighborhood, and the houses were huge with lots of land. There was now a lot more space around the pool table. We didn't have to worry about hitting any walls. The school in that zone was known for its academics. The school I was zoned for was predominately black, and it was known for being hood. I'd heard all kinds of horror stories about fights and gangs, so I was nervous to be going without my best friend. I continued to spend as much time with him as I could before the summer ended. I knew our families' schedules would conflict once the semester started. My parents never volunteered to take me to and from his house, and I knew it would be a burden for his parents to continue to take on that responsibility. We made sure we enjoyed each other's company while it lasted.

The mascot for my high school was a jaguar. The school was massive with a lot of parking. I suppose it was due to many students being within driving age once they're upperclassmen. The way the classes worked was similar to middle school except there weren't pods. Every class was in a different classroom scattered across the building. The lockers were not little boxes. They were quite long. I could stuff my books and a long umbrella in there. PE was only required for one year, and I was glad to hear about it. It was more coed than it was in middle school, so I hung out with the guys a lot more when I was able. Otherwise, I was with the less popular girls who didn't want to play within a large group.

When it was time to play basketball, I was with the girls and guys on one of the side basketball goals singing, dancing, and shooting layups while the others were actually playing full-court basketball. When the players ran down to the opposite side, we'd shoot layups until they started coming back toward our end of the court. I felt more at home with the less popular students. After all, that had been my life the entire time I've been in school. The girls talked about how the guys looked. They talked about how their dicks bounced when they ran up and down the court. I'd make comments every now and then, but I kept most of my thoughts on the inside. Being totally quiet would have probably made them feel uncomfortable.

I still enjoyed watching the girls undress in the locker room. They grew over the summer. My breasts even grew a little, but I was still mainly ass with bigger thighs now. I'd watch the girls' breasts bounce while they ran. I really enjoyed it when you could see their nipples through their shirts. One of the girls mentioned her boob came halfway out of her bra while she was getting dressed, and I missed it. That was probably for the best. Since we weren't really required to play in PE, I didn't have to worry about sweating and needing to shower. I was in and out of the locker room as fast as possible. We all had one requirement for PE that year: to pass a series of exercises. Outside that, we pretty much did whatever we wanted. There was no structure at all. I preferred that over the mandatory playing we had to endure in middle school.

My first encounter with a guy who seemed interested in me was Keith. He was an upperclassman whose locker was close to mine. He was a cute chocolate boy. He was skinny yet toned. He was friendly to me. It was as if something told him to befriend me. We spoke whenever he saw me.

The first time he saw me, he said, "Hey. Are you a freshman?"

I replied yes. He said, "Cool. You're a jag now. Let me know if you need anything."

He eventually took it upon himself to walk me to my locker quite often. He'd just make random small talk. He made me feel protected, and I felt like that was his goal. I've never known anyone who was that attractive to show me attention on that level, so I didn't want to assume he liked me. I was still battling with my feelings of attraction toward the same sex, so I just let this situation with Keith flow naturally. Maybe he was just a nice guy making sure an underclassman was okay. Maybe Shawn knew him, and he asked him to look after me. Either way, I didn't mind. He was a sweet guy. He even carried my books sometimes. If I refused, he just took them from me.

We eventually learned we lived several blocks from each other. He lived not too far from my uncle John Fogg. I walked around in his neighborhood with my cousins, and we'd chat in the street for hours. He'd hug me when I left and tell me he'd see me at school. He never tried to come on to me though. He was respectful. At times, I had thoughts when I wanted him to be disrespectful. On hot days, he would be outside with his shirt off. He had a really nice, chiseled chest and great abs. I just wanted to touch him all over, and I wanted him to touch me all over. The only thing that turned me off was he had a huge belly button. It really stuck out. I tried not to look at it. He hung with thuggish boys, and they had their shirts off too. My hormones were doing the most, but I always fought temptation.

Shawn didn't last long at school with me. He tended to get into trouble a lot. He was always skipping school. One time, I saw him and our cousin in the principal's office sitting on the ground. They were caught skipping school. They were off-campus drinking, smoking, and having sex with girls. Every time I turned around, I thought Shawn would be getting in the car with me when we were picked up from school. I was told he was picked up from school earlier for getting in trouble. Shawn and I eventually talked about his behavior, and it blew my mind. I was told to keep quiet.

He said, "You know I have a different father than you all."

I looked at him puzzled and said, "No. Is David not your daddy?"

"No, he's not. I've known since I was little that he's not my real dad. Mama took me to do a blood test, so she could get child support for me. Your daddy's coworker Charlie is my real dad. Don't you say shit to anyone! If Mama and Daddy wanted you to know, they would've told you."

I was floored. "Is this why you act out so much?"

"Yes," he responded, "because I don't know how to deal with it. Mama and I tried counseling, but it's not helping. I don't like looking at her most times. I'm trying, Sis. I promise. I'm really trying."

Shawn transferred to a different school. Mama wanted to see if a change in environment would help him straighten up his act. Unfortunately, it did not. He stole Mom's car while she was away, and he got caught because he drove the car right into the house. I thought it was an earthquake when it hit.

Eventually, he quit school. He got a job to help pay for the car and house repairs. Maybe he knew he wasn't going to last at my school all along. Maybe he did have Keith looking after me. My mind was all over the place. Why didn't Mama say anything? I wanted to ask so badly, but I knew I wasn't supposed to say anything to anyone. How could she cheat on Daddy with his own coworker? Isn't that a sin? How can she talk about all those people in the church? I battled with the news and unanswered questions on my own.

During my sophomore year, I became an office aide for one of my electives, so I interacted with faculty, staff, and students a lot. I'd assist with keeping the attendance records updated and checking students in and out of school. When the office manager was away, she'd even have me sign passes for students. When parents came to check students out, I'd go retrieve them from their classes.

During one of those trips, I encountered Cole. He was tall, light-skinned, and muscular with full, juicy lips. He played sports for the school. He picked on me to get me riled up. It was never in a manner to where we were fighting. It was as if I was being hazed. It was like that elementary school crush quarrel.

I knocked on the classroom door, and Cole opened it. He stood blocking the door and asked, "What you need, li'l mama?"

I told him who I was looking for. He kept blocking the door and told me the person wasn't in there. I tried to peek in to see if a teacher was there, but he moved in the direction of my eyesight every time I moved. I tried to get around him, and he wouldn't let me. I got frustrated and cussed him out. The teacher eventually came to the door to see what was going on. I gave the teacher the note, cussed Cole out again, and went back to the office.

When I got back, I was heated. The office manager saw it on my face. She asked me what was wrong, and I informed her of the situation. She wasn't having that, so she corrected it immediately.

Cole apologized and let me know he was just playing around. Clearly, I was not for play-play, and I told him I don't play around like that. From then on he spoke to me in a different manner whenever we were around each other. I eventually warmed up to him, and we continued to be cordial when we saw one another. He looked after me from that point forward. If I ever had to get someone from his class, he'd put his arm around my shoulder, walk me into the classroom, and announce who I needed. He would stop the entire class. It was hilarious and embarrassing at the same time.

Lunchtime was a time for me to free my mind. I didn't have to think about schoolwork, and I could socialize with my peers. Due to my parents not being wealthy and having an army of children, I got free or reduced lunch. There were also other things you could buy besides the regular school lunch. There was a window where mini pizzas were sold. Cookies were sold by the home economics class. Candy was sold where we bought school supplies. I rarely got to indulge in the extras, so when my parents or siblings gave me money to do so, it was very much appreciated.

I sat with the special education class at lunch. My cousin was in that class, so I chilled with her and her friends. We were already close because of church. Her step-grandfather was my uncle John Fogg, who stayed near Keith. People made fun of me because I hung with my cousin and her classmates. I didn't mind. They were a great group of people. I was never a popular kid anyway, so it didn't make any difference to me. Even if I was popular, I probably would've still hung out with them. Most people hung with me if they wanted to cheat off of my paper. Half the time they just told me they wanted to cheat and didn't even hang out with me. They'd rather just pay for the services than have to be seen hanging with my nerdy ass.

That was fine with me. I'd rather spend my time with people who genuinely enjoy my company versus people who want something from me all the time. I'd take up for my lunch crew when people talked about them. We'd cuss them out or make jokes about them just like they did us. Due to our always being bullied, we'd dish out our problems among one another to get it off our chests. We'd also discuss popular things such as the latest TV shows and music. We'd talk about the crushes we had on people who we'd probably never get. Some of the crew was already having sex, and I was shocked. I thought about sex, but I was too scared to engage. Masturbating was good enough for now, but it made me wonder what I was missing out on. I wanted to ask detailed questions, but I held back.

Sometimes we'd witness fights in the lunchroom. One guy stood up on the table in the middle of the room talking shit, and a dude came and knocked him right off. I was scared. I'd never seen anything like it. People randomly started food fights, and I'd try to run out because I didn't want to get dirty. Some people sat through all three lunch periods. It was an entire shit show.

During my junior year, I had my first girl crush, and her name was Mandy. She was everything I could ever dream of. She was pretty, smart, and heavily into the church. Her singing voice was amazing. She was in the school choir. I knew my mother would like her due to her religious beliefs. However, I knew Mama would kick my ass if I tried to date her. If she was a dude, she would have been perfect for me to date and marry. I don't even know if Mandy liked girls, but we were extremely close. My mother was very funny about what type of people we should date. She was color struck, and she doesn't care for overweight people. Mandy was brown-skinned, but she wasn't fat.

I wanted to go to prom, but I didn't have a date. Cole and Keith were going with popular girls. Mandy wanted to go to the prom as well, so I told her we could go together without dates. I told her we'd make our own fun. She agreed. I let my parents know I wanted to attend, and my mother told me I couldn't go. I told her I was just going with friends, and I didn't even have a date. She still told me I couldn't go. She said it was too expensive, and she couldn't afford to get me a dress. She also told me I didn't need to be doing those worldly things, and girls usually wind up pregnant after attending the prom. My heart was broken. I informed Mandy I wasn't able to go and told her why. She told me her parents were extremely religious, but they trusted her not to do anything bad. I told Mandy to have the best time of her life and enjoy it for both of us. I eventually got frustrated and no longer wanted to figure out if she was into girls anymore. There was no point if I could never do anything. The life of a sheltered pastor's kid is a complicated one. In addition to not being able to go to prom, I was also not allowed to go to the homecoming dance, after school meetings for clubs I was a member of, or most sporting events. I understood money was tight due to growing up in a large family. Some of my classmates had jobs. I offered to get a job, but I wasn't allowed to do that either. Mama wanted me to focus on my education. I just couldn't win. Brick walls were all around me. All my options were shot down, and I started to shut down.

Besides my crush on Mandy, I had a male crush named Nigel. He was extremely funny and nerdy like me. He was attractive as hell, but he had a big-ass head, big like Bobby's from *Bobby's World* or Stewie's from *Family Guy*. However, I still liked him. He was light-skinned and really tall. He had a pretty smile with straight, white teeth. He had those sharp vampire fangs, and I wanted him to sink them into my neck. *Drain me!* He enjoyed basketball and video games. He talked about how he got new fighting games and an arcade joystick for his birthday. I wanted to play with his joystick. I'd be engaged in the conversation talking about the games Killer Instinct, Street Fighter, and Mortal Kombat.

But in the back of my mind I was thinking about him putting his moves on me. *Finish me! Show me no mercy! Hit me with your ultra-combo!* There was just something so attractive about him. I'd have sexual thoughts about him being between my legs. I'd look between his legs for a dick print, which I spotted a few times. He also had a big butt. I wanted to know what he felt like. I wanted to know what he smelled like. He could've taken my virginity. I wanted him to fuck me so bad, and I knew absolutely nothing about fucking.

One day we were in class making jokes as we always did. I wanted to feel him between my legs and smell him. Looking at him just made me want to rub on myself. While he walked down the aisle, I ran and jumped on his back. He grabbed my legs to hold me up. I wrapped my legs and arms around him. I put my head on his shoulder and sniffed his body. His cologne smelled really good. I got that hot sensation all over my body. I knew it was bad to have this sensation while I was in class, so I slid down off his back. I wanted to slide down something else.

He turned around, smiled, laughed, and went to his seat. I felt that would be the closest I'd get to having him between my legs. Why couldn't I just have sex like everyone else? Ugh! My conscience wouldn't let me be great.

After four years of hard work and not much of a social life outside of school, the end was near. I couldn't believe I was about to graduate. I was not allowed to go to prom. I was too scared to participate in senior skip day. I didn't go on the senior class trip. My mom was too cheap to even allow me to take a senior picture, so I wasn't in the yearbook. Twelve long years of school, and these were my final memories.

Graduating, however, was a memory they couldn't rob me of. My graduation made me feel free. I'd be the second child to graduate from high school. I was so proud of myself. I was in the top ten of my graduating class, which was more than one hundred people. I knew I was smart, but I didn't think I was that smart. I just did what I had to do to progress to the next grade.

My mother told me she'd get me a car if I graduated high school. That was something to look forward to. I guess they wanted to ensure another child would graduate, and I made sure that happened. My parents were so proud of me. Although I didn't do the greatest on the ACT, I received a full scholarship to Normal University and a partial scholarship to UARC. I couldn't believe it. I only scored a nineteen (out of thirty-six) on the ACT, and I still received scholarship offers. I received one from another college in southern Alabama, but I'd never heard of the college. I was already scared to go to college locally, and the southern part of Alabama was too far from home. I couldn't bear moving that far away.

A lot of family attended the graduation ceremony because I went to school with a few cousins. My mother made sure any available church family attended as well. After commencement, I was unable to do the things my classmates were doing, such as eat at particular restaurants or go to parties.

Instead, my family took me to a pizza buffet. I was embarrassed and disappointed. After all the hard work I'd put in, that was all I got. I was grateful to be celebrated, but this was a slap in the face for me. I could understand they needed to spend wisely due to the number of people in our family, but they didn't give me the option to enjoy anything afterward on my own. It didn't cost anything to go to a friend's house for a party. It didn't cost anything to go hang with my cousins who also graduated. I wasn't even surprised with a car when we got home. I went to sleep sad that night.

6

Postsecondary Education

*T*he summer before college was basically nonexistent. I decided to take the full ride to Normal University, which made me a bulldog again. A requirement of the scholarship was that I start school during the summer. Although I didn't want to start until the fall, I accepted. It would have been crazy to reject a full scholarship, which included room and board. I advised Dr. Ennis, the director of the scholarship program, I was from Rocket City, so I didn't need to stay on campus. He advised me it's a requirement so the students can all get acquainted and be available to one another for study sessions and team-building activities. I told my parents, but they weren't exactly thrilled about me living on campus, so I followed along with having a room for the sake of not losing my scholarship, but I still planned on commuting from my parents' house. After all, there was no way for the director to know if I was staying on campus full time.

I was excited to get out of my parents' house, if only part time. This would allow me to test how it felt to get away from them and their rules. However, I was still scared because I had never lived without them. They never let me get a job, so I didn't know what it was like to have my own money. I didn't know what it felt like to take care of myself. I didn't know what it felt like to drive myself anywhere. I was extremely behind in life compared to a lot of my peers. It was time for me to grow up as much as I could without my parents completely freaking out about my decisions.

The first day of orientation was approaching. I had a conversation with my mother concerning the car I was supposed to receive for graduating high school. She told me she didn't have the money to get it yet, but it was coming. When the first day of orientation arrived, she allowed me to drive her Buick back and forth to school. Although I wanted to have my own car, I was happy she allowed me to drive versus someone in the family dropping me off.

I drove across town to get to NU. The campus was huge. I had never been on that side of town before, so I made sure I was early. Due to Dr. Ennis providing a map, I was able to find the building where orientation was held. There were sixteen of us in the scholarship program, and we introduced ourselves. Many students were from parts of Alabama I'd never heard of. We all had to sit with Dr. Ennis to pick out a major and get our class schedules set. Afterward we were assigned rooms and given a tour.

The campus was beautiful and hilly. Walking around was great cardio. After the tour we were dismissed, and everyone went to their rooms. I let my roommate know that I'd barely be there, so she could basically take over. I'd probably only be there between classes. I was hoping I didn't make a mistake telling her the room was hers because she was extremely nasty. She left stained underwear in the middle of the floor. I don't know if they were shit stains or period blood. Either way, I did not want to share a room with her. I instantly requested a different roommate. First impressions are lasting, and I was not about that life. I don't know if she did it on purpose because she may not have wanted me as a roommate, but it worked out in both our favor. Dirty underwear is not a good look under any circumstance.

My second roommate was cool, so I stayed in that room for the semester. We were both nerds, so we got along fine. She really didn't bother me much, and I didn't bother her. Half the time I went home to eat and do laundry. I rarely stayed on campus overnight. On the mornings I commuted from home, it was hard to find parking, so I'd park in the dormitory's parking lot and walk to class. I'd usually go to my room on breaks between classes. My roomie and I watched TV or played video games if we were in the room at the same time. We even studied occasionally. If I decided not to go to my room, I'd walk around campus trying to learn where everything was located.

Learning the campus was a little challenging, but that was expected due to its size. My first goal was to ensure I learned all the shortcuts to my classes. There were plenty of hills to cut through to get to different buildings instead of walking the designated paved routes. Half the time I followed other students to see where they were going. I just had to make sure I didn't fall down any of the hills because some of them were steep. If it rained the previous day, I refused to tiptoe in the mud, so I'd walk the long way to class.

If I didn't know where anything else was, my fat ass knew where the food was. If I wasn't in the cafeterias during lunch, I was at the Oily Fork, a restaurant on campus known for their wings and fries. There was a computer lab next to the restaurant, so after eating, I'd walk to the lab to waste time.

My brother Shawn worked not too far from my school, but our home was across town. From time to time, my mother asked me to take Shawn to work. Since I was driving her car, I agreed. Shawn's shift started extremely early. I was up around five in the morning to get him to work by six. I literally passed my school twice when taking him to work and heading back home. I hated that shit, so

I told my roomie I'd be coming to the dorm early in the morning to avoid going back and forth. The drive was too much, so the decision to just stay on campus after dropping him off worked out.

I eventually got tired of taking Shawn to work, so I decided to stay on campus permanently. On one occasion I didn't want to take him. It wasn't feasible for me to drive across town to pick him up from home and then back to this side of town. My parents had cars. They could take him, or they could let him drive one of their cars. I did a no call, no show with my mother and Shawn. But the following morning I woke up to go to class, and her car was gone. I called my mother to tell her someone stole it. She told me she took it because I didn't take Shawn to work. I felt relieved and upset at the same time. I hung up and went to class. I could not believe she took the time out to come on campus to find her car. She did not know which dorm I lived in, nor did she care to ask about how college life was going. However, she cared enough to get her car. Priorities!

I eventually got the car back. I informed my mother it wasn't fair for her to have taken it because I was supposed to have a car for graduating anyway. I also told her it was not convenient for me to take Shawn to work. She felt that since it was her car, I had to follow her rules. I totally felt what she was saying, and it motivated me to make sure I took care of myself. As a result, I got a job so I could get my own car. I was a cashier at a fast food restaurant around the street from my mom's house. I worked with a lot of people I went to middle school and high school with, so it was fun. Mama always told me she didn't want me getting a job, but she made sure she came by to take advantage of my discount. I was so embarrassed. She came to the window to order something for the whole family: nine hamburgers, nine fries, and nine sodas.

Being a sheltered child, I didn't know who to run to for knowledge about buying a car, so I asked my dad to help. He told me to go hunt for a car. When I found one I liked, he would come look at it. Through my search, all the cars I could afford that we looked at weren't reliable. My mom eventually found out that my dad was helping me find a car, so she told me I could take over the payments on her Saturn, and she would transfer it to my name after it was paid off. Feeling as if I had no other option, I agreed. I was buying my own graduation present. What type of shit was that?

Now I was back on campus with a different car. I parked it at the dorm and walked to class. On my way, I dropped everything I was carrying. A guy saw I needed help because every time I picked something up, something else fell. The wind blew my papers away from me. I was frustrated and ready to cry. I really dislike clumsy days.

He proceeded to help me. I thanked him, and he told me his name was Chad. We kept in touch and went to lunch together occasionally. He was handsome and plump. Outside of my scholarship group and classmates, he was the first guy that I talked to on campus. This interaction made me feel attractive. Someone actually approached me and wanted to keep in contact. One conversation we had during lunch was about roommates. He told me his roommate was inconsiderate, so he asked to be moved to a single room. I didn't even know they had single rooms. As the semester came to a close, I decided I was tired of having a roommate as well. I didn't have a problem with her; she was cool. I just wanted my own space. Per Chad's recommendation, I talked to the resident director about getting my own room. I was approved to move to a room that had a Jack-and-Jill bathroom, which I shared with the resident assistant (RA). I could deal with that. It was better than sharing a bathroom with half the floor. I could also make my room my own. I signed the agreement and was ready to move the following semester.

As time went on, I learned that CollegeClub (CC) and BlackPlanet (BP) were the major social websites being used by college students on our campus. I signed up for both. I created my profiles, added pictures, and explored the sites. There were many people discussing all kinds of topics, from education-related to social events. On day one, a girl named KT messaged me on CC. She was a cute chocolate girl with locs. We conversed back and forth about random things. She asked if I was a freshman, and I confirmed I was. She clearly didn't read my profile because that tidbit of information was in there.

We discussed video games, which was a huge turn on for me. We talked about food, which was also a plus. We realized we had lots of little things in common.

College life was starting to look up. I felt slightly popular. A guy had talked to me during my clumsy moment walking to class. Then a random girl hit me up with an amazing conversation. This was awesome. We arranged to meet for lunch in the cafeteria. We knew what each other looked like from our profile pictures, but we told one another what we were wearing just in case. When I arrived, we greeted by shaking hands and smiling. She introduced me to some of her friends, and we all ate together. We became good friends, and I became a part of their lunch crew.

After hanging with KT for a few weeks, she hit me up one morning on CC. We talked as we normally did about how the day was going, what we wanted for lunch, what game we were currently playing, things like that. She then said she had something to tell me, and I had to promise I wouldn't get mad. I was thinking, *What the hell did this bitch do that's going to upset me? I don't really know her like that.*

I agreed not to get upset. She said she was attracted to me. I blushed and then froze. I'm glad she said this over the chat instead of in person. I sat there trying to gather my thoughts and respond appropriately. I didn't know what to do or say.

As I was trying to think, a message came through, saying, "Hello! Are you still there?"

I stared at the screen for a while. I finally responded to let her know I was attracted to her as well.

She said, "Cool! I'll see you later on at lunch."

I smiled and replied, "See you then."

I immediately logged off. I didn't want to look at the computer or even get another message. I just sat there in awe. I was kind of scared to even go to lunch, but it would be awkward if I didn't show up. I had to proceed as normal, so I walked to the cafeteria from the computer lab. Outside of avoiding direct eye contact, lunch went as normal as possible. It was like our morning discussion on CC never happened. The lunch crew talked about class, their dance team practice, and what was happening around campus. The dance team had a practice that night, and we all agreed to hang out at Tanqueray's house afterward. I wasn't on the dance team, but I graduated high school with Tanqueray, so I was comfortable enough to meet them at her house.

Once lunch was over, I finished up the rest of my afternoon classes. I had nothing but time to burn after my last class, so I went back to my dorm and played Final Fantasy VII for a while. I received a text from Tanqueray letting me know they were done with practice and would be at her house in thirty minutes. I ensured I got to a save point on my game because I refused to start over again by just shutting the system off. I put in too much work. My characters were leveled up. I saved the game, turned off the system, locked up the room, and headed to my car.

Ruff Ryders was one of my favorite rap labels, so I listened to Eve's CD during the ride. It had just dropped that summer, and everyone was bumping it on campus. While bobbing my head to the music, I wondered how this gathering would turn out. I'd never hung with Tanqueray outside of school, and I'd never hung around the dance team outside of the cafeteria. I was excited and nervous all at once. The thought of hanging with KT really had me anxious. I let all the excitement out during the ride because I refused to look like a happy groupie when I pulled up to the gathering. I had to put on my game face.

I pulled up to her apartment, and the music was blasting—there wouldn't be any problem finding her unit. I got out of the car and made sure it was locked with the alarm on. I wasn't used to going anywhere, and I didn't know anything about the neighborhood. My mama just gave me this car, and I didn't want anything crazy happening due to negligence.

I walked up the stairs and knocked on her door. I hoped they heard the knock because the music was obnoxiously loud. I felt bad for their neighbors.

Leonard, the captain of the dance team, answered the door. He said, "Waddup, Ri? Tanqueray is in the shower. We're going to barbecue shortly. Do you want something to drink?"

"Yes, I'd appreciate it. What y'all got?"

"We just made some hunch punch. Can you handle it?"

I looked at him and said, "Most definitely."

I wasn't new to alcohol. When I was younger, Shawn and I were curious. Daddy always went into the utility closet, and we wanted to know why. I was about five, and Shawn was about eight. I was coerced to go into the closet with my brother. We discovered a brown bag on the top shelf. Our bad asses had to climb on the deep freezer to even reach the bag. We both took sips of the mystery drink in the bag. It was downhill from there.

After the utility closet encounter, we finished the remains of Daddy's beer cans and cigarette butts that he threw out. As soon as Shawn was old enough to legally buy alcohol, he brought me some too. This was why I was not scared of the hunch punch.

I grabbed my drink from Leonard, spoke to everyone, spotted KT on the couch, and sat beside her. We all talked shit, danced, and vibed to music until the food was ready. I sat back and thought of how much of a late bloomer I was. Most of my friends did this type of shit in high school, and I was just now experiencing it. I thought I needed to be back home, but I was no longer living at home. I don't have a curfew. Is this what being away from home is all about? Is this what it was like to have lenient, open-minded parents? I liked it.

As it got later, people started to leave. KT, Tanqueray, and I were the only ones left in her apartment. KT and I were still on the couch eating our third helping of chicken wings. This was why I fucked with her. We were both greedy as hell. We talked about food all the time and then ate our asses off. It's the little things that matter most.

Tanqueray looked at us and said, "I'm getting ready to go to bed. Y'all know we have class tomorrow."

KT responded, "Duh! Do you mind if we spend the night?"

She nodded and walked to her room.

I nearly choked on my drink, but I continued sipping to avoid the awkwardness I felt. She really just volunteered me to stay the night at someone's house. That was not in the plans.

Tanqueray came out with blankets. She threw one on the loveseat and the other at us on the couch as she said, "Good night," and walked off toward her bedroom.

We finished our food and drinks and went to the kitchen to clean up. Then KT turned off the lights and headed to the loveseat. She told me I could have the couch since she sprang this on me last minute. I tried to get as comfortable as I could on the couch. I closed my eyes and began to doze off.

A few minutes later, she crawled under my blanket and got on top of me. She whispered in my ear, "Be quiet. You don't want to wake her up. So, you think I'm cute?"

I whispered, "Yes." She felt for my head and kissed me on the lips. My body temperature began to rise. I responded by kissing her back. She started tongue kissing me deeply as she caressed my thigh. She pulled my leg up so she could ease between my thighs.

She whispered in my ear, "Have you ever been with a girl before?"

I thought back to the incident in middle school, but I felt like that didn't count, so I told her no.

She asked, "Do you know what you want sexually?"

I already knew what I wanted to happen. I had fantasized about fooling around with girls for quite some time. It was never anything heavy. I just wanted us to suck on each other's titties and feel on each other's asses. However, that seemed like child's play.

I responded, "I don't know."

My response made her pause for a second; I suppose she was expecting a different one. After processing what I said, she asked, "Do you like the way it feels so far?"

I replied, "Mm-hmm."

"I figured, because I can feel how hard your nipples are." She kissed me and ran her hand under my shirt and played with my nipples.

Jackpot! I didn't realize they were that sensitive. It felt good when I played with them, but someone else doing it was on another level. I started to moan.

She whispered, "Shhhhh."

I tried to tone it down, but I had never experienced this feeling. She proceeded to lift my shirt and bra and used her tongue on my nipples instead of her hands. She swirled her tongue around in circles and then pulled on my nipples with her lips.

I moaned and jerked. I held her head as she made me weaker with every lick and tug.

She got up and said, "We need to stop. You're getting louder. We'll finish this later. Good night." She kissed me and walked over to the loveseat.

I was lying on the couch, stunned. I was still breathing heavy, and my mind was all over the place. I couldn't believe what had just occurred. It was like something out of a porn. Was this real life? I wanted to masturbate so badly. Once I calmed down, I eventually forced myself to go to sleep.

7

College Gone Wild

We woke the next morning, and it was time to go to class. Tanqueray didn't have class until ten, and KT had an earlier class. She didn't have a car, so she asked if she could ride back with me to campus. I nodded.

We headed back, and I turned off my Eve CD and turned on the radio.

She turned the volume down and asked, "How was last night?"

"It was interesting. I never thought anything like that would happen. You really turned me on. It was like something off of TV. You're quite aggressive."

She giggled and then asked, "Don't you stay by yourself?"

"Yes. I'm on the first floor by the RA. We share a bathroom, but I have my own room."

"Cool. I stay by myself too. My roommate moved out. I don't think she liked me, but that's not my business. You should ask to be transferred to my room."

My eyes bugged as I tried to concentrate on getting us safely to campus. I just told this bitch she was aggressive, and now she's telling me she wants me to move in with her.

I replied, "I wouldn't even know how to go about requesting it." I said that to allow a little more time to register what the hell she just said.

She swiftly replied, "Don't worry about it. I'll handle it. This isn't my freshman year, and I know how to get things done around here."

I'm sure my facial expression told on me as I continued driving to campus, it didn't matter; but she was quite sure of what she wanted.

We pulled up to the campus, and I dropped her off just in time for class. She didn't wash her ass or anything. She just took her stanking ass right to class. She didn't even have her books. Bless it! After dropping her off, I pulled up to my dorm to take a quick shower and walk to class. Not washing was not an option. However, the walk to class made me feel like the shower was all in vain. It was so hot that I perspired during the walk. I don't normally sweat, so it made me feel disgusting. Alabama heat is no joke.

The whole time I was in class, I thought about food. Spending the night at Tanqueray's threw my whole daily routine off, which made me miss breakfast. That's what I got for being grown.

Once class was over, we all met at the cafe for lunch as usual. KT advised me that she put in the request for a roommate, and I'd need to confirm it. She told me I should get an email tomorrow from student housing. Once again, I'm sure my facial expression told on me because I was shocked at how fast she got the ball rolling. She was on a mission. During the lunch conversation, we talked about how good the food was at the barbecue last night, and how whoever made the hunch punch was trying to set us up for failure. Tanqueray didn't say anything about hearing noises, so I was relieved. I was sweating bullets thinking she would bring it up.

Either we were quiet enough, she could sleep through anything, or she heard it and just didn't care.

Once I finished with my afternoon classes, I went back to my dorm. I still had not received an email from the resident hall director. I figured it may take another day or so. As soon as I sat on my bed and turned on the TV, there was a knock at the door. I looked through the peephole, and I saw it was the director.

I opened the door, and she asked directly, "Do you want to move in with KaTrina? You just moved into this room not too long ago, so I was making sure the request was legitimate. After all, it didn't come from you, and her roommate just moved out two weeks ago."

I thought, *Who the fuck is KaTrina?* It dawned on me that it had to be KT because no one else talked to me about moving in with them. I was thinking KT was really pushy, but I liked her. It would be cool to move in with her. Hell, I just learned her real name. We knew a lot of the same people. Maybe it would be a great opportunity to get to know her better.

I said, "Yes, I'd like to move in with her. We were discussing it previously, and she said she would get the ball moving on the request."

The director responded, "Okay. Come with me to my office, and we'll complete the transfer. Do you want to move now, or wait until the semester is over?"

I replied, "Now is fine." After all, I really didn't have a lot of things to move. Most things were still at my parents' house.

The director and I completed the paperwork. KT and I both received a confirmation email.

*

KT walked down from her room, now our room, on the second floor, and she helped me move my things to our new residence. I was excited and sad at the same time. I was happy that I was able to be with her, but I was sad that I'd have to start sharing a bathroom with multiple people again. Community bathrooms just seem so unsanitary.

We got my things moved in. Since I had to have everything in place in order to prevent myself from going nuts, I quickly settled into our new space. I put my items where I wanted them. I made sure the bed was made. My next and final concern was hooking up my TV and video game systems. That was my biggest source of entertainment and comfort.

Once everything was done, I said, "I really appreciate your help with all this, KaTrina." I giggled after I said her name.

She replied, "You got jokes. No one calls me that, but I'll let it slide this time."

We then went to the cafe to have dinner.

Dinner was different from lunch. We didn't always meet up with the crew, depending on scheduling. This evening, it was just KT and me, and I think it was done on purpose. We didn't even go to the same cafeteria we normally attended. I guessed this was the ice breaker to discuss our new living arrangements. I was totally wrong. Over dinner, she asked if I wanted to be her girlfriend. I felt it was all moving too fast, but I'd never been in a relationship with anyone, so I was down with it. Given my nonexistent track record, it felt like a once-in-a-lifetime opportunity that I couldn't resist.

From that point, I took the time to let her know what I needed in a roommate. "I need the room to stay clean," I advised, "because I can't deal with dirty panties in the middle of the floor again."

We both laughed, and she nodded.

"My video games are my babies," I ranted, "but you can play them too. However, they need to be treated with care. I don't do fingerprints on my CDs. I don't like people playing on my saved games. I don't like being bothered during game time. I can wear a headset if necessary, so you can watch your TV without being disturbed while I'm playing."

She agreed to those terms. Outside that, I told her everything should be cool. She told me she was a private person, and she doesn't want a lot of traffic in and out of the room. I agreed and expressed I was the same way, and I really didn't fool with too many people to have much company anyway.

When we got back to the room, we resumed from where we left off the night at Tanqueray's. As soon as she closed the door and locked it, she kissed me while walking me toward one of the twin beds. She pulled off my shirt and resumed kissing me. I think she was an aggressive man in her former life. She caressed my back while wrestling her tongue against mine and unhooking my bra.

I began to moan. She stopped, turned on the TV, and turned the volume up. "I forgot that fast. You're about to be loud again," she said.

She just didn't care about my poor feelings. Ugh! Two can play that game. Before she could get back to kissing me, I put both my hands against her chest to stop her. I pulled off her shirt. She was not about to have me shirtless while all her clothes were on. She had on a sports bra, and I could see her erect nipples through it. I pulled her bra over her head and placed it on the floor with her shirt. I played with her nipples with my hands, and I discovered hers were sensitive too. I put the tip of my tongue on her nipple while undoing her pants.

She asked, "Are you sure you've never done this before?"

I ignored her and continued. I slid her pants and underwear down and slid downward with them. She kicked out of her shoes, pants, and underwear. I looked at her hairy pussy, and I got back up to start kissing her. I thought I was ready to give her oral, but I just couldn't do it. Maybe it was the amount of hair that turned me off.

She pushed me down on the bed. She took off my shoes, pants, and panties. She told me to move toward the top of the bed. She got in the bed with me and spread my legs. "Damn! Look at that pretty pink pussy."

The next thing I know, her mouth was on my coochie. She started to lick and suck on my clit. I immediately began to moan. It felt so good. With every tongue lashing, my moaning intensified. The wetter I got, the more excited she got. She slurped up all my juices. She grabbed my titties while eating me out. I held her head in the direction where it made me feel good the most and squeezed my thighs around her head. That's when she really gave it her all. I'm not sure if she got tired of me grabbing her head, but she eventually pushed my legs back to my head and started tongue fucking me. It was everything, but I felt exposed. She was having her way with me. I started fondling my nipples. She alternated from dipping her tongue inside my walls to going back to my clit. I told her I was getting close. That turned her on. She started rubbing herself while eating me out. A few minutes later, I told her I was about to cum. She kept licking and sucking until my love secreted all over her mouth, dripping down her chin and dripping down my ass. A few seconds later, she was busting a nut. She slapped me on my thighs and said, "That was fire. Let's go to bed."

From then on, all I could think about was sex. It stayed on my mind. We fucked like rabbits. She introduced vibrators, and she realized I enjoyed being penetrated. She also knew nipple play was mandatory. She made sure she fingered me or used a vibrator while sucking my clit. That's when I came the hardest. She would use a strap-on while rubbing my clit. She knew all the things to get me going. If I came, she was always sure to cum. It's what got her off every time. I enjoyed riding her while she wore the strap-on. It was easy access to everything, and I controlled the sex.

Once, we got caught having sex. I was riding her in a chair in the middle of the dorm room. My back was facing our window, and KT's face was looking toward the window. There were girls in the dorm across the way looking into our window from a higher floor. My goal was to get my nut. KT wasn't bothered either, so we finished. I honestly think she liked being watched. There was another time we almost got caught during a room check. We had the beds pushed together. She was fucking me hard that morning with the strap-on.

The resident director knocked on the door, saying, "Room check." She used her key and opened the door.

KT jumped off me, pulled the beds apart, and jumped under her cover. We weren't caught fucking, but KT was caught trying to get things in order before she fully got under her cover. I don't know if the director saw the strap-on or not. I also didn't care in this incident because I didn't move. I liked to fuck, and whoever witnessed it was just going to witness it.

KT eventually told me she wanted some reciprocation. I had always fantasized about messing around with a girl, but I never exactly knew how it was going to go down. KT led the way with everything, so I followed her lead. She wanted me to eat her pussy. I wasn't opposed to it, but her bush was just overwhelming. I didn't want to hurt her feelings, and I understood where she was coming from, so I worked with it. I felt like I was back at our first time in the dorm room.

I stared directly into the bush. I used my fingers to keep the hair out of the way, and I ate her pussy. Once her juices started flowing, I started getting into it more. I saw why she liked it. She tasted sweet. I'd play with myself while sucking on her pussy because I was so turned on. I wondered if I tasted like her. Only one way to find out. I inserted my fingers inside me and put them in my mouth. I did it again and put my fingers in her mouth. I put my fingers inside her, and she pushed my hand down. She told me she prefers not having anything in her. Duly noted. I knew the fact that I came turned her on, so I proceeded to sit on her face. I let her lick me while I licked her. She knew how to make me cum, and she succeeded. Shortly after, I was still eating her out and she started to cum. I lapped up her juices and kissed her until our juices were devoured between the two of us.

Our sex life had been amazing. However, KT came to me with an odd question. "This lady hit me up on CC. She's a very attractive older woman, and she wants to have a threesome. Are you down?"

I was shocked by the question, but I was also a horn dog. So I told her we could do it. She gave a big grin. She went to the computer and showed me a picture of the lady. She was Hispanic and very pretty. That night, we drove to her house. It was a passionate interaction. It was a heavy foreplay session. The lady had a foot fetish. She enjoyed rubbing her feet on different parts of our bodies. She used our feet to rub her clit until she came, and she did multiple times. She would put our toes in her pussy. She even asked us to do it at the same time. I left a huge hickey on her neck, and she had to go to work with a turtleneck on while it was warm outside. At that point, I felt like I was a sex fiend. We left the woman's house and headed back to campus. I went to sleep thinking about sex.

All day I dreamed about sex. I couldn't stop thinking about it. I just wanted to nut and make other people nut. I thought about how KT was hit on by someone on CC. That was how we met, and that was how we had a threesome with someone. I logged on to CC. I was really shy, so I didn't hit anyone up. I waited for someone to message me. A girl hit me up, stating she lived on the third floor. She wanted to fuck me with a strap-on. I told her I had a girlfriend and she was in class. I told her we only did things together. She didn't want to wait on KT. She said I was the prettiest girl she'd ever seen, and she wanted to make me cum really hard. I was intrigued, so I invited her over to my room. I felt safer in my room for some reason. She was cute, but she was bigger than I expected. She also had a blonde afro. I was horny, so I let her fuck me. She did make me cum, but it wasn't thrilling. I decided not to tell KT about it because I felt bad for doing it without her consent.

Now I knew CC and BP were sites to get to know people in more than one way, I was hooked. I had signed on and met plenty of females to have sex with. There was one incident where I felt like I was being set up. Depending on how one looked at it, it could have been considered a bad and potentially dangerous situation.

A girl named Rachel hit me up, asking me to come to her house to freak. Of course I was an addicted whore, so I went over. She appeared to be completely high on something, but I didn't care. She was talking slow, and her mouth was juicy, as if she was drooling. We fooled around for a minute and started having oral sex. She was stroking my insides with her fingers while licking my clit, and it was feeling really good.

All of a sudden, someone came out of the closet. It was her best friend, Ben.

Ben said, "Are you gonna let me get some too?"

I was a bit disturbed. I loved how a strap-on felt, so I was curious to see how it felt to be with a man. I nodded for him to join.

Rachel got up and let Ben take her place. His dick was already hard from watching, so he put a condom on and slowly slid inside me. He felt amazing. A strap-on didn't throb inside me as his dick did. His strokes felt different. Feeling his balls slap against me was a different sensation too. The smell and feel of a man between my legs were different than a female. After several minutes of pounding, the good sensation started to hurt. He was fucking me hard for a long time, and I just wanted him to hurry up and nut. He could tell I was hurting by the look on my face. He asked if I wanted him to stop, and I nodded. He told me he was still going to make me cum. He told Rachel to ride his dick while I rode his face. Rachel and I kissed each other and sucked on each other's titties while we rode different parts of Ben. I came on his face, and I went back to my dorm sore that evening.

After days passed, I couldn't hold it in any longer. I confessed to KT that I was a sex addict, and we needed to break up. I told her about all the sex I'd been having. She was upset, but she understood. She knew I was a virgin when we met, and I never got to have my hoe phase. She also understood that she introduced me to a lot of this, but she wanted to stay together. I told her I didn't want to be in a relationship because I'd continue sleeping around. I told her I might as well be single since I was acting like I was anyway. Although she was hurt, she understood. We went our separate ways. I decided to move off campus with my brother Jack.

After my breakup and moving off campus, I told Shawn I was gay. He was shocked. I don't understand why because he made fun of me my entire life about being gay due to playing with boys more than girls. He always talked about how I'd rather play with his toys than with my Barbie dolls. However, he said it was all jokes, and he never thought it was really true. He told me he loved me and supported me regardless. I had him tell my parents and everyone else that I was gay because I didn't know how to relay the information. My parents told me I wasn't raised that way. They told me I was straight, and this was just a phase. I knew it wasn't a phase. My urge to be with girls didn't change. I was told I was going to hell. I was prophesied to in church in front of the entire congregation, who said I was going to die and burn in hell if I continued dating females.

So I stopped attending church. Church was supposed to be a safe place, and I was made a target. I was made the topic of many sermons. I don't know why I was surprised because I'd seen this behavior the entire time I'd been attending my mother's church. I guess I thought she would never do me that way. I started questioning my life. I considered suicide. I realized I was battling who I was because I was trying to please my parents instead of myself. My mother was just fine with my cousin in Tennessee being gay. He was damn near her best friend. I didn't understand why I was treated differently. However, I snapped out of it. I had to be comfortable being me.

8

Moving Forward

*A*fter the breakup, I continued with my shenani-gans. I was still on the chat sites for the purpose of finding people to have random sex with. After all, I didn't need a time period to be depressed and bounce back. I broke up with her. It was back to my regularly scheduled program. I connected with one of the cheerleaders, Tanisha. We kicked it off and on throughout a year's time. She stayed in an apartment close to campus, which was convenient. Anytime our schedule allowed, I was over there getting eaten like Thanksgiving dinner. I always returned the favor. She kept that fat rabbit smoother than a baby's bottom, so I didn't mind serving her up. She was really cute and thicker than a Snicker. I'm sure it was probably due to all the exercises cheerleaders had to endure. Her thighs and ass were amazing. I wish I had the discipline to be that toned. Mine were just jiggly, but I liked it. Apparently, she liked it too as well as all the other people I've fooled around with who kept coming back for more.

Sex with Tanisha was always amazing. She sang to me in the

mornings when I spent the night, "The best part of waking up is RiRi in your bed."

Outside of our sexual escapades, we hung out with her friends. They were all upperclassmen. We'd just sit around watching TV, talking shit, and joking. Tanisha loved her soap operas, so we'd watch them. She occasionally had snacks or ordered something from a restaurant. If she ordered food, it was usually a pizza or a box of chicken. If it was snacks, it was random items like potato chips and dips or cookies. Being the whore that I was, I vibed with a lot of her friends, which led to me fucking around with some of them.

I messed around with one of them on a regular basis. Her name was Terrica. We even fooled around on Tanisha's couch. Tanisha was completely fine with it. I honestly think they all fucked around with each other, but I had no way to prove that. I never asked them about it either because that wasn't my business. They discussed how they went scouting for fresh meat on campus. I'm quite sure that's how I was targeted. They called it the freshman hunt.

As time went on, Tanisha eventually got a girlfriend, Frannie, so we had to stop having sex. I respect boundaries, but that really made me sad. I guess I can't have it all. I was being greedy and selfish, and she deserved to be happy.

Tanisha eventually introduced me to Frannie, and we all became close friends. Frannie was extremely young. Not even old enough to be freshman hunt meat. However, there was nothing but love and respect for their relationship. We'd all just hang out at their apartment and have a great time. Frannie eventually moved in with Tanisha. She left her hometown to ensure she could devote more time to their relationship. She also wanted to go to Normal University. One of our mutual friends told Frannie that I used to have sex with Tanisha. I honestly don't know the motivation behind revealing that fact, but I wasn't bothered by it. I had nothing to hide. Frannie eventually confronted me about it. Due to my conscience always getting to me, I told her the truth. I told her we did mess around quite often. Tanisha, however, denied it, and she continued to lie about the situation. Apparently, she had things to hide. She told Frannie that she didn't recall us ever doing anything sexual. Frannie called us on three-way to clear the air. Tanisha continued to stick with her story of us never messing around. I stuck with my side stating we did. From that point forward, Tanisha and I stopped being friends. Frannie respected me for being honest. We became extremely close. They eventually broke up, and after Tanisha finished school, she moved back to her hometown. I never heard from her again, and she eventually stopped reaching out to Frannie.

Since the adventures with Tanisha ended, I was back on CC to find my next venture. I felt the need to find someone to fill that void. Terrica went to the military, so she was no longer an option.

I received an invite to a party by Earlene, one of the many girls I had sex with. I hadn't talked to Earlene in quite some time, so I was shocked to see the invitation. We messed around once, and I was done. The thing I remembered was that she'd had two orgasms. I didn't let the lack of communicating with her afterward hinder me from accepting the invite, so I went to the party. After all, she clearly didn't mind sending it, so I was totally on board with partying with her and her friends. Who was I to turn it down?

There were a lot of people there. I noticed quite a few I'd had sex with. Most people probably would've felt awkward, but I was just fine. I'm not ashamed of anything I've done, and it's not like I was walking around wearing a T-shirt announcing everyone I'd slept with in the room. It was about having fun with good people, cocktails, and food. Earlene always kept liquor on hand even if there wasn't a party. She was known to make your liver quiver when you hung with her.

When I arrived, she pulled me to the side. She asked why we never hooked up again. I told her I was too busy being a whore, and it was nothing personal. She laughed and completely understood. Several guys and girls were trying to hook up with me that night, so I had my pick of the litter.

One girl, Lynn, was extremely interested in getting to know me. She was attentive and ensured she was around me all night. If she wasn't beside me, she was in a close enough distance to where she could keep an eye on what I was doing. When she saw other people talking to me, she stared at us until we were done, and she'd come back over to where I was.

I thought that shit was funny, so I'd fuck with her by moving around a lot. I was all over the place talking to many people. That usually happened when I got drunk. Otherwise, I was good keeping to myself if I was sober. The liquor made me social. Lynn was from out of town. She made sure we exchanged numbers, and we made sure we stayed in contact. During one of the games we played, one of Earlene's friends told me she wanted to have sex with me. I told her I wasn't interested. She continued to ask, and I continued to decline. She proceeded to say that I've messed around with everyone else, so I might as well give her a chance. All I could do was laugh.

Lynn came back to Rocket City a couple of weekends later. We stayed at Earlene's house. They were good friends, which in turn had me back in connection with Earlene on a regular basis. Apparently, Lynn started out at Normal University before transferring back to a university in her hometown. Earlene and Lynn met their freshman year at NU, and they remained friends after Lynn transferred.

As time went on, Lynn and I decided to start a relationship. She was happy with me, and she wanted to make it official. I agreed to being her girlfriend. I traveled to her hometown, Plainsville, three hours away. On one of my visits, an old lady ran into my car, and I got heated. Lynn blamed herself for the accident because it wouldn't have happened if I didn't have to visit her. After I calmed down, I assessed the vehicle, and there was no damage. The rest of that visit was pleasant. We continued the long-distance relationship for a few months. Distance started bothering me, so I moved in with her in Plainsville. Driving back and forth can take a toll on you. I knew if I didn't move, I would have cheated. I enjoy sex too much.

In order to ensure I didn't completely fuck over my education, I enrolled at Plainsville University (PU). The only thing I had left to do to complete my transfer was submit my official transcript. However, I think the admissions office worker at NU had a crush on me because she was doing everything in her power to prevent it from happening. She was giving me every reason in the book to stay. Of course, it didn't work. I was determined to leave. NU already had a shitty computer science department, and the students had to rotate sharing computers in the lab every Tuesday and Thursday when classes were held. Half the class was always left observing versus doing the work. It was hard to gain experience programming once a week. I knew it was past time to move on, and Lynn helped with the opportunity. Once the semester ended, I left NU and my hometown, which was all I'd ever known.

When I arrived in Plainsville, I got a job near the apartment we secured before I moved. My coworkers were nice and extremely country. They made working there fun. It was in a call center doing customer service for a wireless carrier. I had already worked in a call center for a media company, so I felt this shouldn't be too hard. This was my first apartment, and it was away from my family and friends. I was finally able to see what it would be like to live with someone off campus who wasn't family. I was somewhere that had my name attached to a lease agreement. I was able to see what it was like to have bills. I learned how they were supposed to be split and paid on time. I learned how to cook. It was a totally new experience for me.

PU was also a new world. It was a predominantly white school, and everything was so organized. I didn't have to fight for a refund check. Everything was done on time. Most things were done electronically. We had to have our own laptops, so there was no big fuss about not having enough computers in the lab. They provided all the software needed for classes. It was available for download through the web portal. I had some classes with people from my hometown who I hadn't seen since high school. We'd hang out at their apartment from time to time. Catching up with them was beautiful. It's always good to see familiar faces. I was loving this new place I called home.

As classes began to get harder, I started fucking over my time at PU. I lost focus and stopped caring because I wasn't used to getting bad grades. I stopped going to the majority of my classes. I'd only go when it was time to take a test. I passed one class during second semester, which was for students who were failing. That was the only class I attended. Outside of that, I started to focus on my newfound freedom, which included partying and hanging with my new friends. I was always at the club when the Black Greek Letter Organizations (BGLOs) threw a party. It was the closest feeling I got to HBCU life as when I was at Normal University.

When I wasn't in town, Lynn and I traveled often to visit one of her best friends, Gwen. At the time, Gwen was staying in New Orleans to get her MBA. We went to visit her for Mardi Gras. I was still under twenty-one, so I had to stand outside of clubs they went into that were for people twenty-one and older. It was cool because they made sure I had liquor, and they didn't stay long. They told me about what went on inside of the clubs, which was a bunch of sexual activities.

Gwen gave no fucks about me being with Lynn. She tried to

have sex with me on many occasions. While we were in a club that I could get into, she was grinding on me and putting her hands in my pants. I was not used to this type of behavior from best friends. She was literally rubbing my pussy on the dance floor until I pulled her hand out of my pants. The level of disrespect was shocking.

Once Gwen finished school, she moved to Peach City, where we were able to see her more often. On one visit, one of her friends was in town for a party, and she wanted to fool around. I talked to Lynn about it, and she was down with it. We had an orgy with many people at the party in Gwen's bedroom. Gwen was not included, and that gave me a sense of great satisfaction due to her being oblivious to boundaries. I believe Gwen sat out because she had a girlfriend, and she didn't want to test those waters. Her girlfriend was there, and she was not about that life. It all worked out for me.

While I'd been enjoying my life away from Rocket City, Shawn, being my best friend, started to miss me. We were used to being around each other quite often. He said he wanted to come up with the kids to visit. Lynn was cool with it.

When he arrived, we got him and the kids settled in. Afterward, we all went to the pool. It's amazing how my niece and nephew both knew how to swim, and I still didn't know. I don't even like getting my face wet, so I probably will never be able to learn. I freak out when I wash my face in the shower. That rinsing part is a doozy.

During our conversation at the pool, Shawn told me he met his half-sister. I was puzzled, and I'm sure my face showed it. He told me he knew he had a different father earlier in life. I vaguely remembered him relaying this information when we were in high school, but I don't think I committed it to my long-term memory due to us never talking about it since then. I also didn't think he would go out trying to meet anyone. I digested the information as best I could.

"Does Daddy know?" I asked.

He said our father knew. I felt sick to my stomach. I was so lost. This story just brought reality back to the forefront. Inside, I wanted to cry, but it wasn't the time nor place for sadness. I prefer not to let children, or anyone for that matter, see me sad. I feel like it's a sign of weakness. We continued enjoying our time at the pool with my niece and nephew. We discussed the similarities between Shawn and his sister. He said they both have the same bottom lip, and it runs in their family. He told me his father is still alive, and he planned on meeting him one day. I was happy for him, but I was also sad for our father. This was a strange situation, but I supported Shawn in what he needed to do to feel complete.

*

Later that summer, I started to get tired of being in my relationship. Lynn started working at the same place I did. That wasn't a big deal. She was able to be closer to home, and it allowed her to make more money. The problem was I was with Lynn all the time. We lived together, worked together, had lunch breaks together, and even had the same friends with the exception of my friends from PU. She questioned why I was keeping secrets from her that one of our mutual friends trusted me with. She felt she should be in the know since we were all friends.

I started to feel like I didn't have my own identity. It drove me crazy, so I broke up with her. She is an amazing person. I was just overwhelmed. After that, our relationship was rocky for a few weeks. It was awkward living with someone I had just broken up with. We had to get through the end of the lease without pissing each other off.

As time went on, we were able to be friends. We handled living arrangements the best way we could. We upgraded to a three-bedroom apartment and moved in with a mutual friend, Winnie. Winnie helped us transfer our things over from one apartment to the next, which was across the parking lot and up a hill. Winnie was extremely silly, and she kept everyone laughing. While we carried the couch over to the new apartment, she made a joke that caused me to laugh and drop the couch. We laughed until we were able to gather our composure to complete the move. There were a lot of items we had to move running from one building to the next. In addition to that, we also had to get Winnie's stuff from her mom's house, which was fifteen minutes away. In the end, it was all worth it.

Once we all settled in, things got a lot better. Lynn and I no longer shared a bedroom. She could have whatever company she wanted without wondering if I was going to be in the bedroom or not. I could do the same.

I was fucking around with a few people from school. One girl, Joanna, was really cute, and she was also a huge geek. That turned me on. Beauty and brains have always been a thing for me. It took us a while to warm up to each other because she seemed wet behind the ears when it came to sex. Clearly, sex was a big thing for me. One night, we were at a gathering with friends, which consisted of a lot of lesbians from the basketball team, and the topic was about what we all liked to do sexually. One girl mentioned that she enjoyed eating ass. Joanna was completely floored by this statement, and she asked me if I liked to do it. I told her I didn't have a problem doing it, but I could live without it. She giggled and blushed like a little schoolgirl.

The conversation got extremely wild. Two girls discussed how they liked both holes filled while being eaten out. It seemed like an innocent conversation. However, there was secret information that the girls discussing the topic had done that to each other prior. One of the girls was in a relationship, and her girlfriend was present. Once the girlfriend put all the pieces of the puzzle together, a huge fight broke out.

Winnie, Joanna, and I left as soon as we felt safe enough to move. All three of them were fighting. They were throwing anything they could get their hands on, including a coffee table. Once they were done, it looked like the Tasmanian devil had attended the party. From that point forward, I never hung out with the lesbians from the basketball team unless it was on an individual basis.

The following night we had a party at our apartment, and Joanna was in attendance. The occasion was due to one of Lynn's exes coming into town. We had lots of food and drinks. Joanna pulled me into the kitchen. She pulled up her skirt and didn't have any panties on. She told me to eat her ass. She had clearly been thinking about the conversation from the previous night, and it apparently had her intrigued.

I'm not one to disappoint, so I did. I thoroughly enjoyed it, and she did as well. It got her really wet, and it made me excited. She told me to stop before anyone decided to enter the kitchen. I washed my face in the kitchen sink, swished a cocktail around in my mouth, and joined the rest of the party in the living room.

Lynn's ex said she wanted to stay the night, but she didn't have a change of panties.

"Just flip them," Joanna said. We all looked at each other, puzzled. Joanna then explained she should just turn her current underwear inside out.

We all laughed our asses off, and Joanna's nickname from then on was Just Flip 'Em. She would make that comment after I ate her ass. That clearly meant this bitch flipped her underwear inside out when she stayed the night over someone's house and wasn't prepared to stay overnight. Ugh! Oh well. What's done is done.

As the lease was nearing its end, Lynn was also nearing the end of her final semester. My college life was pretty much nonexistent at this point. I was focused on working and partying. Once Lynn graduated, she told me and Winnie she was moving to Peach City. She said she completed her goal of graduating college, and she needed to go somewhere that would allow her to put her degree to use. Plainsville did not offer her any opportunities.

She gave us two options concerning our living arrangements. She said we could move to Peach City, and she would make sure we had somewhere to stay until we got on our feet. She told me she felt responsible for me since she pulled me from my hometown and family, so she wanted to extend the offer to come along. Winnie could've moved back home, but Lynn wanted to give her the opportunity to get away from the small college town. We had the option to renew the lease without Lynn as well as find a different complex to stay in if we decided we wanted to continue to live with each other. Winnie and I thought this was a great opportunity to get out of Plainsville, so we packed our shit and moved to Peach City. Onward and upward!

Peach City

elocating to Peach City was an easy move. Even though we weren't all moving to the same location, we put our belongings on one moving truck. Lynn moved in with Gwen, which wasn't a good place for me to stay. I'd never feel comfortable alone with Gwen. She does the most. I don't understand how you can want to take advantage of your best friend's girlfriend. She continued to come on to me a couple of times after Lynn and I broke up, and I politely declined.

With that being said, it would have been extremely awkward for us to live together, so I stayed with Earlene. Winnie technically moved in with us too, but she was never there. I had already built a friendship with Earlene once we started hanging out again from the party, so it wasn't a big deal. She was happy to have the consistent company of a roommate. It actually helped us to become a lot closer. She's one of my good friends now. We both love to eat and drink, so it's always a fun time. She's a neat freak, and I am too. I never gave her any issues with paying bills on time. We didn't invade each other's space. I didn't keep a lot of company outside of people I was fucking and dating. She's actually one of the best roommates I've ever had. She loved to cook and entertain. She always had people over. It was like party central, or it was like going to my grandma's house. I was always guaranteed to see someone over there. When I wasn't in the mood, I'd stay in my room to get some peace and quiet. Sometimes people came to my room to hang out because they weren't in the mood to party hard all night either. We'd relax while watching TV or playing video games. Other times we'd just chitchat. I'd encourage them to go back to the party because I didn't want to seem like I was taking people from the event. Also, too many people would end up in my room, and that annoyed me. At times, I'd just suck it up and tell everyone we, including myself, needed to go mingle downstairs.

My first girlfriend in Peach City was someone I had already messed around with when we traveled from Plainsville and stayed with Gwen on the weekends. It was a chick I met from a gay dating site. I'm wondering how many people actually went on dates from there because it seemed like everyone just wanted sex, which wasn't a problem for me. Anyhow, it was a trip we made for Thanksgiving. I didn't want to travel to see my family in Alabama because we don't get together as we used to after my maternal grandmother passed. Everyone did their own thing. Gwen had just moved into her new house, and Earlene said she would cook for everyone.

That afternoon, most of our friends were out and about seeing people they knew in Peach City while Gwen and Earlene were getting things prepared for the holiday. I didn't know many people in the city, so I stayed behind and got on the chat site. That was my norm whenever I got bored, so it was nothing new.

I got a message from Marquel. It's like people instantly flock to your inbox when they see you're from out of town. I guess they like new meat. They feel like it's something no one else in town has ever had. Kind of like the freshman hunt. We exchanged messages about what we'd do to each other. We exchanged nudes, and we were both impressed by what we saw. She finally asked me to come over, and my hoe ass went right on over to her apartment. We fucked around, but I wasn't thinking it would go any further. It was a wham-bam-thank you-ma'am. We gobbled each other up like we were the Thanksgiving entrees. She made my gravy boat drip.

I didn't live there at the time, so my mind was far from a relationship. When she saw on the chat that I was back in Peach City, she quickly hit me up. She noticed that my listed state changed from Alabama to Georgia. She invited me over to catch up. I went back to her apartment, and we messed around again. She advised she did not want to lose contact with me again. She wanted to make it official, so we dated for about six months. I enjoyed the sex. She was very pretty with long, silky, curly hair. She always kept it pulled back in a ponytail. She was toned, and she drove an old pickup truck that you thought Fred Sanford would've owned. It looked like it belonged on a farm. She was from the West Coast. She said her dad gave her the truck, and she didn't want to part with it. She worked at a nightclub managing strippers. She was a stud, and all the females were after her. I'd visit her job occasionally, and she'd bring me drinks. Many females rolled their eyes at me.

The relationship was going well until the upcoming summer when Marquel decided she wanted to go to Miami for Sizzle, and I wasn't feeling it. I already felt funny about our relationship because she worked at the club with a bunch of strippers who would do anything for a nice size of cash. Sizzle was known to be a place for hooking up. She was adamant about going, and she didn't need to go for work to manage the strippers. It would have been a leisure trip. She made her decision to go, so I broke up with her. I wasn't about to stop her from living her best life. There are plenty of fish in the sea. Go do it up in Miami, boo. See you on the other side.

I decided I should try to be single for once in my life, but that didn't last long. I swear I need help. I don't know how to be alone. I started going out with someone else for a few months, and I broke up with her on her birthday, at her birthday party, which we had at Earlene's house. I was trying to hold out until after the party, but the relationship wasn't going down the path of making me happy. She was a depressing young lady. It's like nothing would go right in her life. Earlene called her Schleprock because she had the worst luck. She reminded me of Eeyore because she was always gloomy. It was like she had a dark cloud hanging over her head. She was very pretty, but clearly, looks aren't everything. She seriously needed to sit on someone's couch to let everything out. Lastly, her vaginal lips were longer and meatier than I preferred, so I knew we wouldn't last too long if I had to continue performing oral sex on her. The only roast beef sandwich I ate was from Arby's. Earlene continued to be friends with Schleprock, so, unfortunately, I had to see her every now and then because Earlene loves throwing gatherings and inviting everyone in her address book. Earlene is the friend collector no matter how she met them. Within our group, a few of our friends had to encounter their exes at Earlene's functions. These were usually unpleasant surprises because not everyone's relationships ended on a good note. Schleprock always got excited when she saw me. I was cordial, but I could never go back down that road again.

After staying with Earlene for a little more than a year, I decided to move to my own place. I told Winnie I was getting ready to move, and she advised that she wanted to stay with me. We found a three-bedroom townhouse apartment in the city. It was really nice. The location was amazing. It was near a beautiful golf course. The community was gated. Access to every major interstate was within ten minutes away. There were plenty of stores, restaurants, lounges, bars, and clubs. It was the perfect location.

One of Gwen's friends wanted to move in with us, so Winnie

and I agreed that was fine. Winnie knew her better than I did, and I trusted Winnie's judgment. I actually stayed single the entire time I was in that apartment. I had the time of my life. I always had a girl over, but I promised myself not to commit to anyone. It was about getting that orgasm. It was about enjoying my single life to the fullest. Winnie and I were back into our old routine like when we stayed in Alabama. You couldn't keep us separated long. We were always going out to the clubs. We got so drunk one night that I couldn't even get the front door open. I sat right on the front stoop laughing until I could gather myself to get into the house. Once I got the door open, I lay across the threshold and laughed some more. I eventually made my way up the stairs into my room and passed out.

Although I was having an awesome time with Winnie, Gwen's friend didn't know how to give people space. She was always in my room for something, and she had no need to be in there. I know when my things are out of place, and that bitch was always in my room. I know Winnie wouldn't violate me like that because we'd stayed together before. Gwen's friend also tried to shove the cable bill down my throat when I told her I didn't want or need cable. I refused to pay it, and I told her she could shove that cable box up her ass. She also had the nerve to be upset because I had my entertainment center and video games upstairs in the bedroom, and there was no entertainment center in the living room. That was a personal problem.

I moved to another apartment by myself once the lease was up. I couldn't handle it anymore. I made sure I gave ample time for them to find another place to stay before I left. I wasn't going to leave them high and dry. My new place was a nice one-bedroom townhouse loft. I enjoyed looking down from my bedroom into the living room. It was an enjoyable space. I continued living the single life there as well. I didn't have to worry about anyone going into my room anymore unless I invited them in.

A Puerto Rican girl lived in the complex, and I met her on the chat site. We fooled around as often as we could. She liked to nut multiple times, and she always had to do it in different positions. I wanted her to cum on my face.

She said, "You gotta work harder for this next nut, and you gotta do it from a different angle."

Outside of the sex, I wanted to entertain myself the way I did during my childhood. I wanted to play more video games, but I wanted something new. I wasn't going out as much with the girls since I stayed by myself. I wanted to get myself a PS3 as a present for getting my own place. It would keep me occupied at home, so I wouldn't have to go out spending money in clubs all the time. I didn't want to pay full price, so I went online searching for used ones. I found one on Craigslist. The price was really nice, so I contacted the guy to get the details. He advised me that he was selling it cheap because he charged it to his credit card, and he was going to dispute the charge. His son messed up in school, and he felt he didn't deserve to have a PlayStation any longer.

I was a little hesitant because I didn't want it to come back on me as stolen by them tracing the serial number when I registered it online and played. However, I hopped on the deal and picked up the console that night. When I arrived at his apartment, he still had on his work clothes. He answered the door in his light blue scrubs. He was a doctor. He worked for the hospital around the street from where we both lived. He asked me to sit so we could go over the details of the sale. He was pouring himself a glass of wine, and he offered me some. Of course, I accepted. While sipping, he went over everything about the console and plugged it in to show me that everything worked. He demoed both games he bought for it. I told him I was good with it, and I handed him the money. He grabbed the money and my hand, pulled me in close, and started kissing me. He was attractive, and I was tipsy from the wine, so I went with it.

When he pulled out his dick, my jaw could have literally hit the floor. It was huge. Apparently, my face spoke for me, and he told me he'd be gentle. He made sure I was comfortable in every way, from the foreplay to easing his way in until he felt me open up to him. I enjoyed how he preheated my oven before he shoved his meat in. He made me cum twice. I left with my PS3, and I never talked to him again.

One night, I was back on the chat site, and Marquel popped up. She just happened to see me and felt the need to hit me up. Of course, I fell for the spiel she gave about missing me and wanting to see me. I went to her crib, and things picked up from where they left off. We were staying over each other's apartments. I no longer stayed in town. I was in the suburbs.

Marquel got tired of traveling to my spot, so she had something up her sleeve. A few months later, she got my belongings from my apartment, and I moved in with her. The things we didn't take we put on Craigslist to sell. Everything was sold at a great price, including my washer and dryer because Marquel's unit didn't have the connections.

My second time around with Marquel was shaky within two months. I kept catching her chatting and flirting with other girls online and via text messages. It made me uncomfortable. I had already been in a previous relationship where Lynn and I messed around together, but Marquel never let on that she was into that. To address my concerns, I asked her if she wanted to mess around with other girls as a couple or be in an open relationship. She didn't want to do either. She couldn't see another person touching me.

However, she continued to sneak around and hide things that I'd always find. I got upset one night because I caught her chatting sexually with another woman. I locked her out of the apartment via the deadbolt and door chain. She left and came back later that night. I opened the door for her because I had time to think about my next move. I told her whether she liked it or not, we were now in an open relationship. Since she didn't want to lose me and still wanted to continue her sneaky behavior, she agreed. I started seeing females on the side, and I'd let them all know I was in a relationship. Marquel, on the other hand, continued to lead people to believe she was single. Whatever works!

After all the years that had passed since my Normal University days, I finally paid my car off. I was so excited by this accomplishment. That was an extra $325 a month in my pocket. Once I paid it off, the car started acting up. I took it to the dealership, and I was advised it had a transmission problem. It's like these cars are rigged. A major problem just happened to pop up once I paid the car off. What type of shit was that?

I contacted my mom and told her I needed her to transfer the title. I needed a reliable car, and I couldn't trade in a car that wasn't in my name. She refused to do so. She said she felt the car was worth repairing. Mind you, I talked to the Saturn dealership, and Saturn was going out of business. The dealership advised it wasn't worth repairing. My stubborn mother still refused. After putting more than $10,000 into that car, she traveled from Rocket City to Peach City to take the car from me. I was devastated and hurt. I felt betrayed and sick to my stomach. I now had no car. I got fucked over by my mother again concerning a vehicle. How in the hell was I supposed to get back and forth to work?

Thankfully, Marquel taught me how to drive her car, which was a manual transmission. She sold the junkyard truck for a fly-ass coupe during our breakup period. She let me drop her off at her job, and I drove myself to work in her car. On days where she was off, she took me to work. When I got off, there were times when I had to sit for hours until she was able to come to get me. However, she was working hard doing side hustles to ensure we got a second vehicle. She made enough money to buy a used car for around $5,000. It was a piece of shit, and she drove it versus giving it to me. Her commute was closer to her job, and she wanted me to drive the reliable car.

From that day forward, I knew I'd never ask my mother to purchase or cosign anything for me in life. Driving that manual transmission was a challenge, but I was extremely grateful for the sacrifices Marquel made to allow me to drive it. The apartment complex we stayed in had a hill. The first time I drove it, I stopped at the stop sign at the top of the hill. I began to pull off in first gear and rolled all the way to the bottom of the hill. I was so thankful there was no one behind me. After a while, I got the hang of it.

As time moved on and more items accumulated in the apartment, Marquel decided she was tired of apartment living, and she wanted us to buy a house. Buying a house was a big move, but I trusted her. We weren't getting any younger, and a house is the ultimate dream. It's better to start paying toward something in our name versus paying toward someone else's property. I didn't have an issue with that, so we decided to go house hunting.

The process was draining. The realtor showed us houses we didn't like. Grant programs we applied for kept falling through. I had a breakdown and cried because of all the complications we were having. Marquel and I also couldn't agree on a location. I wanted to stay in the suburbs, and she wanted to be in the city. We eventually found something she really liked in the middle of the hood. We just happened to run across the For Sale sign while driving by with the realtor. We took a look at the house and fell in love. The inside was amazing, but the neighborhood was not. I compromised. I wasn't a stranger to hood life, but I didn't want to live in it for the rest of my life. The sellers really wanted to get rid of the house, which should've been a red flag. We didn't have all the money needed to close, so the seller ate the costs. He said most of his properties were in Florida, and it was hard to manage the one in Georgia. With that being said, the closing went successfully.

We were now homeowners of a nice four-bedroom, two-and-a-half bathroom single-family home near downtown. There was plenty of room to entertain. We bought the house during the time the president was giving out $8k for first-time homebuyers. We were able to furnish the entire home. One of the rooms was made into a media room, so I could have my private time playing my video games. When I wasn't playing video games, we'd watch movies. The kitchen and living room were all an open concept, so it was easy to entertain. The family was welcomed. We had a fully furnished guest room. This was an upgrade from Marquel's one-bedroom that she moved me in. Unfortunately, we were victims of break-ins three times. Marquel freaked out because I was a nervous wreck. They took two of my vintage gaming systems. I was heartbroken and felt violated. To help ease my mind, she amped up the security system to include installing burglar bars and doors, cameras, and getting two dogs.

Shawn came to visit quite often. He and Marquel got along extremely well. Maybe it was because they're the same zodiac sign. Shawn's journey had been interesting when it came to dating. He's bisexual. I had him tell our parents that I was gay, but he's been holding his secret in for quite some time. I felt slightly betrayed, but it's not like I came out right away. He told me he was dating a guy, but the guy, Dee, stayed in Ohio. I'd done a long-distance relationship before, so I knew how it could work.

One day he was having a conversation with Dee while Dee's aunt was around. Our last name, Fogg, came up in the conversation because they were talking about families since Dee is originally from our hometown.

Dee's aunt, Caroline, grabbed the phone. "Is your last name Fogg?"

"Yes," Shawn replied.

"Is your mama's name Cheryl?"

Shawn's response yet again was yes.

"Your siblings are my siblings. We've been looking for them for years. My daddy is Tobe Campbell."

Shawn was shocked. He immediately told me of the situation once he hung up with Caroline and Dee.

10

Taking it All In

I was devastated when I heard the news. I was in a daze. It felt like a bad dream. I cried uncontrollably every time I thought about it. Marquel couldn't believe what was going on, and I could understand why. She had never heard of this type of shit happening before in real life. She was used to seeing crazy shit like this in movies and on talk shows like *Maury* and *The Jerry Springer Show*.

Supporting me in this situation was new to her, but she did the best she could. She'd ask if I was okay, go do her day-to-day activities, rinse, and repeat. I always had what I needed before she left the house, including meals. I was not in a position to cook. Hell, I didn't even want to go to work. I preferred to be alone while I was sad, so her lack of being present more than normal was just fine. She still had to live her life. I usually didn't see her until it was time for bed where she would hold me and let me know everything would be fine. The claims that my alleged family were making seemed farfetched to her, but she supported me in confirming the truth as long as I didn't let it consume me. I agreed because my whole demeanor changed. I felt myself getting depressed, and I didn't even know the truth yet.

While Marquel was away, Shawn continuously checked in on me. That's what besties are for. He told me how he and Dee hit it off. He apologized that their relationship opened up this can of worms. However, he felt it needed to happen. Everything happens for a reason, and it was time for us to start researching this allegation. He gave me Caroline's phone number, and I reached out to her immediately.

Caroline told me she was glad I called and gave me the breakdown of everything she could recall. They all lived in Rocket City until her mother moved them to Ohio. She and her siblings wrote letters to Tobe when he stayed with us, but my mother sent them back, advising them not to send anything to her house anymore. My mother was always rude to them when they tried contacting Tobe in any way, shape, or form. Any phone number they called from she blocked. She expressed how Tobe made sure his kids knew about me and stressed how much he loved me, but he had to respect my mother's wishes of not being around since she already had a family. I thanked Caroline for filling me in on what she knew, and I told her I'd contact my mother and be back in touch.

I hung up with Caroline and took in everything she told me. I had to gather the courage to call my mother. I needed to figure out what I was going to say, because my mother didn't play around. I was honestly scared to call her, but I knew I had to get this off my chest. It was eating me alive, but I braced myself and called her.

Her response was exactly what I thought it would be. She said, "I don't know why she would say some shit like that. Tobe ain't your daddy. David is your daddy. You know better."

That made me feel at ease. I didn't see any reason why my mother would lie about who my real father was. I thanked her for letting me know. I apologized for calling about something this crazy.

I called Caroline back, and I told her there must be some type of mistake.

Caroline said, "It's true. If you don't believe me, go to the court office and request the child support papers. Daddy was paying child support for all y'all."

I paused. I asked, "All of us?"

She said, "Yes. You, Marcus, Lyndon, and Rodney."

I was in shock all over again. I thanked her, and I told her I'd call her back. I hung up and started crying. This made the allegation bigger than what I thought it was. I informed Shawn of what I was told. I didn't want to relay the information to my siblings, so as usual, I let Shawn report the news.

After Shawn told our siblings, Lyndon and Marcus went on a mission to get things cleared up. They got copies of the child support papers from the county courthouse. They read me the information over the phone, but it was too much info being relayed. I wanted a copy for myself so I could study it. I called the courthouse to clear up some things, for the documents didn't say there was a DNA test done. It only stated he was found to be the natural father.

I asked the clerk what that meant. She read me the information listed on the judgment and then said, "Based on these documents, it sounds like Tobe is legally your father. It shows the judge ruled him the natural father, and he paid child support for you and your siblings."

I immediately started to cry with her on the line. I couldn't hold it back. She apologized, and I could hear in her voice that she felt bad for me. There is normally a cost per page to send the documents, but she said she'd mail them for free. I guess my crying pulled at her heart strings. My intention was definitely not to get the documents free, but it worked out in my favor. That prevented me from having to mail a money order or check to the courthouse. Through my sobbing, I provided her my mailing address, and I thanked her for everything. She advised me to contact her if there was anything else I needed.

After that crying spell ended, I knew I had to call my mother back to let her know there was evidence supporting Tobe being our father. I played a few scenarios through my head on how she would react. I knew this one wouldn't be good. She just told me Tobe isn't my father, and now I had to call her back stating something is showing differently. I was basically calling her a liar, and that is considered disrespectful in my mother's household. It's just like cussing her out.

I finally got up the courage, and I called her again. She gave me the same answer as before. I asked, "Why was he paying child support then?"

She responded, "He owed me money for things in the church, such as the church van I got him, so I sued him for child support."

I was naive and trusted my mother, so I believed her. It didn't make sense, but I knew my mother was good for taking people to court to get what she was owed.

I thanked her and called Caroline to advise her of what my mother said. "My daddy didn't have a church van," Caroline said. "He owned a painting business, and he had his own van he used for business, which had nothing to do with a church. Tobe is your daddy. Your mama even named her church after his. His church was Spiritual House of Salvation, and your mama named hers Real Spiritual House of Salvation."

I thanked Caroline, and I called my mother again immediately. I told her everything Caroline said, and she replied, "That woman better leave my kids alone. That ain't your damn daddy. I know who I've slept with. How are they going to tell me who I've slept with?"

I agreed with my mother and told her thanks again. However, a memory came back from years ago. This made me remember when I went to my cousin's funeral in 2012.

My maternal aunt by marriage said, "I haven't seen you since you were little. Aren't you Tobe's daughter?"

I told her, "No. David is my daddy."

Why did she ask that? Was she being messy?

Some of my maternal uncles heard the news concerning Tobe being my father. They sent a message through Shawn. They said we should do a DNA test. I was wondering how in the hell we could do that. Caroline told me Tobe is deceased, so I couldn't do one with him.

I remember the year he died. My mother went to the funeral with Andy, my eldest sibling, but she didn't ask the rest of us to go. We never went anywhere my mother went unless we were invited. That was just a rule of the household. I researched how to do a DNA test if your parent is deceased. I found information on siblingship tests and hit up Caroline to see if she was open to taking one. She agreed, and I told her I'd pay for everything. I got her shipping address and ordered the test. A few days later, she received the kit and mailed off her sample. After a few weeks, the results came back that we were not related.

Caroline felt something wasn't right. She felt as if she gave a bad sample. I thanked her for doing the test and relayed the information back to my mother.

Mama was extremely confident and said, "I told you. DNA doesn't lie. Tobe is not your daddy."

I thanked her and told everyone else who was involved. My siblings were relieved. Marquel was elated that this madness was finally over. I was happy too. The situation had completely stressed me out, and it put a strain on my relationship with Marquel.

Right when I was fine with the results, my maternal uncle told me I should get another test done. I guess I got excited too fast. This caused me to get antsy all over again, for he seemed quite sure that David wasn't my biological father. I wanted to throw up, but I couldn't.

"I don't know how to be supportive in this situation," Marquel said, "I've never had to deal with anything like this in my life." She left the house to get some air.

I cried and called my brother Marcus for comfort. He and I had already done a genealogy test to find out what we were mixed with. We always felt we were mixed somewhere down the line, and it turned out to be true. With the genealogy test, you also get DNA matches. He asked our dad, David, to do one, so he could help clear the air. Our mom refused to let that happen.

He then asked Uncle Saul, but he gave an excuse about being too sick to take the test. He then told me to ask our alleged half brother to take the test. Our alleged half brother's name was also Tobe, but he went by Bud. I asked Caroline to reach out to him. She gave me his contact info. I called him, and he agreed to take the test. We purchased the DNA kit and mailed it to him.

Marquel felt we needed a getaway. She wanted to get our minds off day-to-day life to include not thinking about waiting for the DNA results. She didn't want to think about any of that stuff. We decided to take a trip to Vegas. It was my first time going. I knew I was going to be wasted like they were on *The Hangover.* However, I wasn't. It was pretty boring. Marquel didn't want to do the fun stuff I wanted to do. It was cool. I compromised. We went to a lot of shows. We walked the strip, and I made sure I stayed intoxicated. We ate at a lot of good restaurants, and I saw one of my old college buddies who was a veterinarian in Vegas. Overall, it was a good trip. It just wasn't the wild trip I had set in my mind.

Marquel decided to go out one evening when I didn't feel like it. I wanted to stay in the room to relax. I don't like gambling, and I didn't want to walk around looking for things to play to possibly lose money. She left her tablet on the bed, and my nosy ass went through it. I found a video of her having a threesome with girls in our bed. When Marquel got back, I had the tablet opened with the video playing. She looked like a deer caught in headlights.

The bitch was caught again. I told her it was over. She acted as if it was the end of the world and started begging. She told me she loved me, and she didn't want to separate. She said if I broke up with her, she was going to jump out of the hotel window. I didn't want her killing herself, and I did still love her, so I told her we'd work it out even though I knew she wasn't capable of changing. We cried ourselves to sleep in each other's arms.

Once back in Georgia, I resumed playing the waiting game. I was waiting for another alleged sibling's DNA results to come back. While I was dealing with finding out who my real father was, Marquel was dealing with filling the hole I placed in our relationship. Although we decided to stay together, she started dating someone, Tamia, who hung out with my ex, Lynn. They all went to the same gym. Marquel claimed they were just workout buddies, but something wasn't adding up. Something just didn't feel right to me. They spent entirely too much time together. It ain't that much working out in the world.

My car auto-connects to our phones when they're within range. One morning, I got in my car to leave for work, and Marquel's phone connected. Instead of just disconnecting the phone and driving off to work, I went through the call and text log. Lo and behold, the girl's info showed up multiple times over multiple days for months.

All kinds of thoughts ran through my mind. *These bitches have been fucking for a long time.* I wanted to beat the shit out of Marquel. I turned the car off and went back into the house. Marquel was still asleep, but I woke her ass up. I confronted her about it, and she advised our relationship had been on pause ever since I found out about the possibility of having another father. She said it was her way of dealing with it. I was already an emotional wreck, and this made it worse. I wanted to shut down and get back into bed, but I didn't. I had to ensure I made money to keep the bills paid. After this occurred, Marquel and I decided it would be best for us to separate. I advised her it would be wise if she moved out. She agreed. She left, but she didn't move any of her things out. She was still coming around because she still loved me. I told her she needed to move her things, and she didn't.

One evening, she asked me what time I'd be home from work. I told her the normal time I always got home. That was a really weird question for her to ask. I logged into our security cameras and saw an unfamiliar dog playing with one of our dogs. I immediately told my job I wasn't feeling well and needed to leave early. This bitch had the nerve to bring Tamia to the house. They had left to go the gym, but Tamia's dog was there as well as some of her belongings.

I fucking snapped. The girl's car was parked outside. I honestly wanted to fucking slash the tires and key the car, but I didn't. Instead, I may have done something much worse. I took the girl's keys and eyeglasses that were left in our bedroom on the nightstand, and I smashed them with a hammer. I took that fucking dog, and I placed it in the trash can at the end of the street. I called Lynn and told her what was going on because I felt so much rage. I felt like I was going to kill Marquel and Tamia when they got back to the house.

I called Marquel and let her know what I had done. Lynn stopped by and got the dog out of the trash can. Shortly after, Marquel and Tamia pulled up. Tamia couldn't leave because her keys and key fob were destroyed. Her blind ass couldn't see without her glasses. I was looking at her and Marquel from the top of my porch with a hammer in my hand. Marquel eventually calmed me down, and I told her she had to go. She took Tamia back to her place of residence, which was Tamia's friend's apartment, and they left her car on the street. Marquel was upset with me because she had to buy Tamia another key, key fob, and glasses. Those glasses were expensive because they were prescription. Tamia had something fucked up going on with her eyes. Not my fucking problem. It's called karma.

Marquel was still on her bullshit when she got back to the house. I told her I was tired of seeing her in the house while she was dating someone else. I told her she needed to move her shit out, so she had no reason to come back. She eventually made an agreement with Gwen to stay in her rental property.

Marquel and some friends moved furniture out of the house while I was at work. She took things that she didn't even buy. I was completely done. She was on my phone carrier's family shared plan. Since we weren't a family anymore, I cut her phone off. I didn't want to be on the same bill with someone who was fucking my best friend's friend. Let that bitch get her a phone. I don't play that shit.

When Marquel got off work that night, she got mad and kicked a hole in the bedroom wall. I guess she thought that was supposed to scare me, but I wasn't bothered. I told her she needed to pack her shit, and I wasn't playing. She said she needed her phone for work, and she wouldn't leave until it was turned back on. I called the phone company to have it turned back on. The next day, she went to work. I went to the hardware store, bought new locks for all the doors, and changed the locks. I called the phone company and had the phone turned right back off. If that bitch was going to kick a hole in anything else, it would be from outside.

Of course, she was pissed. The next time she came by the house, she lost it. She retaliated by trashing the outside of the house and taking property from out of the crawlspace. I was at work and watched it all unfold via the cameras. The look on her face was priceless when her keys didn't unlock any doors.

As soon as time allowed, I filed for a restraining order, but it was denied. The judge stated it's also Marquel's property, so she can't be found guilty of destroying her own things and stealing from herself. Marquel then retaliated again by getting Tamia to place a restraining order against me. I didn't understand what the restraining order was for. I laughed at the court case because there was no evidence that I'd bothered that girl. Tamia said I was stalking her social media pages. The judge said I had the right to because she was dating my girlfriend. The judge was not happy with me putting the dog in the trash can. I laughed about that too, and the judge said it was not funny. The dog survived the trash can incident, but it was later run over by a car at Marquel's new residence that she rented from Gwen, in which she paid rent by allowing Gwen on her flight rights.

Like my mother, I must have the last word. I wrote Marquel's job and sent proof that I was doing her work because she could not add and subtract military time. I had access to government documents that I shouldn't have been able to view. I also informed them that Gwen wasn't her domestic partner. She was giving Gwen her companion pass in order to have a place to stay without paying rent via cash. After the court situations and the letter to her job, Marquel finally left me alone because she didn't want to put her government job in jeopardy. After all, if she messed up Gwen's flight rights, she wouldn't have a place to stay rent-free.

Now that Marquel couldn't get back into the house, she wanted to arrange to get the rest of her possessions. I told her she should have moved her shit when I told her. A mutual friend talked me into letting them come over to retrieve some of her stuff. It went totally left because she was trying to take shit that wasn't hers, and I called the police. The cops came and advised me to give her fifteen minutes to get things out of the house. They would not let me go in while she gathered her belongings. Once I went back in, I noticed she took a lot more than she should have. I was pissed off. However, she still couldn't grab her things within fifteen minutes. She said we'd arrange for her to get the rest of her things. I told her she had forty-eight hours to get the rest of her stuff, which I placed on the back deck. She retrieved what she wanted from the items. The rest she threw all over the backyard. The following trash pickup day, I made sure it was all placed in the trash can ready for pick up.

As I continued going through the house, I ran across more of her possessions. I ensured they were also picked up on trash day. She didn't take them, so she shouldn't miss them. Besides, she took high-priced items that she didn't purchase. It balanced out. All material possessions can be replaced, and it's not like she paid rent. She had the money.

11

Numb

ud's DNA results finally came back. Tobe Campbell showed up as close family. I jumped straight up in the bed and started screaming and crying.

My current girlfriend, Imani, looked at me and asked, "What's wrong?"

I tried to calm myself so I could answer her. "Bud is showing up as close family. It's true. He's my brother. Tobe is my father."

I started shaking and crying. I couldn't believe it was true. I thought it would be just like the previous DNA test I did with Caroline, but this was not the case. My whole life has been a lie.

Although it was early in the morning, I had to update those who I wrapped up in my search. Shawn was staying at my house at the time, so I went to his room and told him.

"I'm sorry. I know how it feels to learn you have a different father, so I'm here for you if you need me," he said.

We hugged, and I thanked him for being there for me.

Next, I reached out to my brothers and let them know the rumors were true. Marcus wasn't happy. He logged into his account so he could see the results with his own eyes. He had to work that morning, so he said he would deal with it later. He needed to be able to function during his shift.

I contacted Bud and told him the results were in.

He said, "Yeah, I saw it. I told you it was true. We all knew already."

I thanked him for taking the test. I contacted my mother and woke her. The conversation seemed like a waste. She was still saying it wasn't true. "I don't understand how one DNA test is right, and the other is wrong. Something isn't adding up."

I told her I'd look into it. I researched the siblingship test I took with Caroline. It indicated it's best to do the siblingship test with a mutual parent in order to produce definitive results, but you can try without the mutual parent. That's what threw the test off with Caroline. I didn't read any of that when I ordered the test. I just saw a siblingship test and ran with it. The other test is autosomal, so you don't need a parent. It automatically pulls DNA from both sides. I relayed this info to my mother, and she still denied it.

Caroline! I needed to call Caroline. I called her and advised her of the results, and she was happy to hear it. She kept beating herself up about probably taking the other test wrong, but I told her none of that matters now. We got the proof we needed to confirm our kinship.

As time went by, I corrected the paternal side of my family tree. I removed David as my father and listed Tobe instead. I listed Bud and Caroline as my siblings. This started to make things real. As I completed the tree, DNA matches that I couldn't figure out previously started to make sense. All these second and third cousin matches I was wrecking my brain with were now easily connected to my tree via my paternal side. It was mind-blowing.

I let my mother know of these connections, and she was still in denial. I talked to Imani about how I felt like I was having an identity crisis. I was in my thirties and just figuring out who my biological father was. That's crazy. I told her I was going to change my last name. She supported my decision.

I called my mother and let her know. I felt like she knew Tobe was my father, and she didn't want to admit it. Not only was I changing my last name because I felt it would help me identify with who I truly am, I was doing this as a way to get my mom to feel guilty and confess. I figured she would tell the truth and request that I keep my current last name. Sadly, she didn't fall for it.

Her response was, "That's fine. You're grown, and it's not my business. I'll let your daddy know."

It was totally her business because she was the reason I was going through this bullshit. I was crushed, but it pushed me to go ahead and immediately start the process. I completed the necessary paperwork at the courthouse. I submitted the newspaper article stating I was changing my name. I was nervous that my mother would see it and object to changing it. I knew she didn't read Georgia news, but I was paranoid. I checked the paper every day to make sure the article ran with no issues and no one responded. I made it to my court date with no hiccups. I went through with changing my name from Henrietta Fogg to Henrietta Campbell.

Once mom was aware that it really happened, she was upset. Apparently, her response about me being grown wasn't really what she meant. We both were calling each other's bluff, and I pulled out the big joker. She would get really upset when I called home and "Henrietta Campbell" showed up on the caller ID. She said it upset my father to see it. I didn't think about how he felt in the situation, so I had a conversation with David when my mother wasn't around. I knew that would be the only way to have a meaningful conversation with him. Ultimately, he was sticking by his wife's side. He claimed he was my biological father. However, I felt he knew the truth as well. Tobe stayed with us for years. How could he not know?

After about two months, I met Caroline and the rest of my siblings. All my paternal sisters are in Ohio, so I caught a flight to see them. I was nervous and scared. Even though these were my siblings, they were total strangers. However, my family is important, so I made myself get this awkward, initial meeting over with.

My sister Denise picked me up from the airport. She got out and helped me get my things into the car. She hugged me, told me how cute I was, and took me to Caroline's house where I was staying for the visit. When I got there, Caroline and Whitney, my other sister, welcomed me with open arms. After we all greeted one another, they filled me in on family info. I have three sisters and a brother on Tobe's side. They showed me a picture of Lyndon visiting Ohio when he was little. I never even knew my mom went to Ohio with Lyndon. I guess I was too young to pay attention to that. They showed me pictures of our father. They showed me that he kept all our crib cards when we were born. He had copies of the same pictures my mom had of us from our birthday parties when we were little while he stayed with us. It now made a lot of sense why he was in a lot of the pictures. David wasn't even present in some of the pictures. Taking this in was overwhelming.

Caroline had a huge dinner for me, and I was able to meet most of my nieces and nephews. My cousin Dee even showed up. I truly appreciated the experience and good time that they showed me. Caroline's husband made sure I got everything I wanted from food to alcohol, and he gave me a tour of the city.

When I got back from Ohio, I made sure I told my maternal family everything I learned, and I made sure I documented all the names into the family tree. My maternal siblings were floored by the news. It made them want to confirm their biological fathers. All my maternal siblings, except Andy, did the DNA test to confirm who their fathers were. Andy didn't want to do anything to cause my mother to look at him differently. He was staying out of it.

Once the results came back, we were able to confirm every-one's fathers. The information on the child support documents is accurate. All children listed were Tobe's children. Shawn already knew who his father was, and the DNA matches on his side were additional proof. Jack's matches confirmed that David was his biological father. He was relieved. We advised our mother of this news, and she denied it. Needless to say, this has been a devastating blow to the family. We had all been living a lie. It divided us, and my mother blamed me for it. Instead of taking responsibility for her actions, she played the victim. At the end of the day, I was willing to be the bad person so I could live my truth. DNA doesn't lie, but people do.

I went back to Rocket City to meet as much family as I could on my father's side. My aunt Cierra was the first aunt I met. She was extremely honest and funny. She also loved to have a good time. She educated me on everything she knew about my mother and father. She told me how they came to my house for church. She told me how my mother did her hair as well as her mom's hair. She told me David knew everything, and he was just respecting my mother's wishes. She advised me that my real father had play dates with us until David got fed up and requested the visits stopped. Sadly, I don't recall any play dates, so I must have been very young when this was going on. She told me Ms. Bernice Crim picked us up for play dates to meet my father.

All this information had my jaw on the floor. She told me how my mom keyed my father's car. She advised me how everyone in her family saw my mom as part of their family. She showed up to everyone's funeral.

Aunt Cierra said, "Whenever you're in town, you can just pull up. I'm always at the house. I'll cook for you. If you need to stay overnight, you can sleep here. I'm so glad I'm able to see you again. I haven't seen you since you were a little girl."

While I was happy to obtain all the information, it still all seemed like a bad dream. I wanted to wake up, but it was reality. While I was at Auntie's house, Bud stopped by to meet me. He looked just like our father. We talked about family history, but it was more so about illnesses that ran in the family. He educated me on many people having diabetes, and he told me to exercise and eat healthily. This was a lot to take in.

That evening my aunt threw a huge gathering for people to meet me. She cooked a lot of food and played music. We ate, drank, and danced like I've never done with family before. My mother's side doesn't do these types of gatherings. I was able to meet aunts, uncles, and cousins. Marcus came by to meet family, and he asked questions he needed answers to. Lyndon eventually stopped by for a short time as well. Rodney didn't want to be bothered by any of it.

When I got back to Georgia, I had a lot of time to try to process this new wave of family and information. I tried to find ways to cope, but it was really tough. My emotions were up and down. Some days I was just fine, but other days I was a wreck. I've asked my maternal siblings if they were willing to go on Iyanla Vanzant's show, *Fix My Life,* so we'd have some family healing. They all agreed but felt our mother wouldn't participate. I could totally see her not being involved. If she actually agreed to do it, I could see her causing a scene and walking off. Iyanla would probably need her life fixed after dealing with us.

I reached out to my mother and let her know we needed to talk as a family about Tobe being our father. Once again, she advised it was not her business, and she didn't need to talk about anything. I probably needed to sit on a therapist's couch to put everything on the table, but I didn't think I was ready to face it all, especially if the source of this matter was not going to be involved.

Instead of getting the proper help, I became addicted to genealogy. I spent hours searching who I really am. I try to figure out every possible DNA match. I try to extend my tree as far as I can. I've spent nearly $1,000 on genealogy research. By research-ing online and asking family members questions, I discovered some things that I was happy about, as well as things that have devastated me.

On a good note, one of my DNA matches won *America's Next Top Model*, Cycle 3, in 2004. On the opposite side, I think my dad's paternal grandfather may not be his biological grandfather. I did tons of research trying to figure out who it really is but had no luck.

I also found out Ben, from the threesome during my college years, was my paternal uncle. When I went to Caroline's house, she mentioned him and showed me a picture. I was so sick to my stomach. Not only did I have sex with my uncle, but it was in a threesome. Yuck! I really wish I'd turned him down. Every time the family talks about him, I cringe.

Brent, the guy who crushed on me in middle school, is my paternal first cousin. When Aunt Cierra told me we were kin, I spoke with him on the phone. I asked if he remembered me, and he didn't. I told him how we walked home from school together, and it still didn't ring a bell. It was many years ago, so I completely understood.

Glenn, also from middle school, is my maternal third cousin. I had no idea. My mother didn't really take us around any of the extended family. She knew who Glenn's mom was, but we were never taken around them. I notified Glenn of our kinship, and he was shocked and excited.

The guy, Keith, who walked me to my locker in high school, is my paternal third cousin. I let him know we were related, and he knew immediately when I told him who one of my first cousins was. Although with Keith, I'm not quite sure if we're biologically kin due to this mystery of my dad's real paternal grandfather. If anything, we're step-cousins, which is still a connection. A girl who I have followed on social media for years is my distant cousin on my mother's side. We were so excited when we found out our DNA matched. It's highly possible that a female from a couples' trip Imani and I went on is my maternal cousin. I've also found that Marquel, my ex, and I have mutual cousins, but I don't think we're related. Her cousin had a child with one of my paternal cousins. I guess they like to keep it in the family. I wondered if Marquel ever got word of my results that Tobe is my real father. She and I don't talk, but Shawn communicated with her after our separation. My genealogy search is endless. There are enough DNA matches and secrets to keep me busy until I die. I wake up every morning checking to see if I have any new matches. It's an addiction that takes up tons of time, but it's also educating me and others. I think I use that as an excuse not to get help.

Although I've accepted the fact that Tobe is my biological father, I think it will always feel like a bad dream that I can't awaken myself from. I'll continue to keep in contact with my newfound family, and I'll continue meeting as many newfound family members as possible. The last name change randomly freaks me out. When people call me by my new last name, sometimes I cringe. Other times I'm okay with hearing it. I even feel funny when I write it sometimes. Some of my friends still call me by my former last name, and they immediately apologize when they realize they've done it. I tell them it's fine.

Fogg is still an important name for me because my stepfather is an amazing man. He raised five children who aren't biologically his. He will always be my daddy. People who knew Tobe will say I look like him when they see me. My paternal aunt Thelma tells me I look like my daddy every time I see her. My maternal uncle told me if I ever have any doubt of who my father is, all I need to do is look in the mirror. I showed Lynn pictures of my siblings, and she says I look more like them than my maternal siblings. Denise gave me a picture of Tobe when he was younger, and I look just like him. I've always thought I looked like my mother's side since I didn't look like David. I didn't know any better, so that's what I ran with.

When I see my stepfather, who I still call Daddy, I want to cry. It makes me wonder what type of marriage or quality of life he has been enduring. Fifty-plus years of marriage and more than half the kids aren't yours. That's heartbreaking. The man who fathered the kids lived in the house, and David just ran with it. Tobe didn't father just one of the kids, he fathered four. I was too young to understand what was going on at the time.

I want to wake up from this bad dream, but it's my current reality. My maternal siblings are all struggling in their own ways. Even the ones who aren't Tobe's are struggling with this awful nightmare. Instead of being addicted to sex, I'm now addicted to genealogy. I've tested at six different genealogy sites. I guess things could be worse. I could still be addicted to sex. I could be addicted to drugs. I could be into committing crimes. I could be gambling. There are all kinds of other things I could be doing to make myself feel better.

Sometimes, I feel like I should end it all and go see my father on the other side, so he can answer all my questions. Maybe he knows who his paternal grandfather is now that he's on the other side. Maybe he'll tell me why he never told us who he was as we got older. Maybe he'll give me all the closure I desperately require and desire.

But instead of taking the easy way out, I choose to be strong. I choose to live another day.

Some days are good. Other days, I'm just numb.

About the Author

Brian Mackenzie is a native of Huntsville, Alabama. He is a proud alumnus of James Oliver Johnson High School. He obtained his B.A.S. in Technology Management from Clayton State University, in which he is an active member of its alumni association. He currently works as a Quality Assurance Specialist for a well-known real estate software company. In his spare time, he enjoys video games, reading, and genealogy.

Printed in the United States
by Baker & Taylor Publisher Services